"You can't marry Stevenson."

Alan ground out the words. "You don't love him!"

"How do you know?" Ebony said, using her fingers to comb her tangled hair back from her face.

"Because you're incapable of loving any man," he stated harshly.

Her short bark of laughter was half disbelieving, half mocking. "Certainly not a man like you!"

His blue eyes blazed for a second before adopting an expression of cold contempt. "Then why keep on going to bed with me?"

MIRANDA LEE is Australian, living near Sydney. Born and raised in the Bush, she was boarding-school educated and briefly pursued a classical music career before moving to Sydney and embracing the world of computers. Happily married, with three grown-up daughters, she began writing when family commitments kept her at home. She likes to create stories that are believable, modern, fast paced and sexy. Her interests include reading meaty sagas, doing word puzzles, gambling and going to the movies.

Miranda Lee is the author of Hearts of Fire.

Books by Miranda Lee

HARLEQUIN PRESENTS
1711—BETH AND THE BARBARIAN
1728—MARRIAGE IN JEOPARDY
1737—AN OUTRAGEOUS PROPOSAL

The Hearts of Fire Series:
1754—SEDUCTION & SACRIFICE
1760—DESIRE & DECEPTION
1766—PASSION & THE PAST
1772—FANTASIES & THE FUTURE
1778—SCANDALS & SECRETS
1784—MARRIAGE & MIRACLES

Don't miss any of our special offers. Write to us at the following address for information on our newest releases.

Harlequin Reader Service
U.S.: 3010 Walden Ave., P.O. Box 1325, Buffalo, NY 14269
Canadian: P.O. Box 609, Fort Erie, Ont. L2A 5X3

Miranda LEE
Mistress of Deception

Harlequin Books

TORONTO • NEW YORK • LONDON
AMSTERDAM • PARIS • SYDNEY • HAMBURG
STOCKHOLM • ATHENS • TOKYO • MILAN
MADRID • WARSAW • BUDAPEST • AUCKLAND

ISBN 0-373-11791-4

MISTRESS OF DECEPTION

First North American Publication 1996.

Copyright © 1993 by Miranda Lee.

All rights reserved. Except for use in any review, the reproduction or utilization of this work in whole or in part in any form by any electronic, mechanical or other means, now known or hereafter invented, including xerography, photocopying and recording, or in any information storage or retrieval system, is forbidden without the written permission of the publisher, Harlequin Enterprises Limited, 225 Duncan Mill Road, Don Mills, Ontario, Canada M3B 3K9.

All characters in this book have no existence outside the imagination of the author and have no relation whatsoever to anyone bearing the same name or names. They are not even distantly inspired by any individual known or unknown to the author, and all incidents are pure invention.

This edition published by arrangement with Harlequin Books S.A.

® and ™ are trademarks of the publisher. Trademarks indicated with ® are registered in the United States Patent and Trademark Office, the Canadian Trade Marks Office and in other countries.

Printed in U.S.A.

CHAPTER ONE

'I PRESUME you'll be going to the wool fashion awards tonight?' Deirdre Carstairs asked her son over lunch.

'Unfortunately, yes,' was his cool reply.

'Why "unfortunately"? Fashion is your business, after all.' And your life, she added silently, and with some irritation. Alan had always been a workaholic, but lately he was worse than ever, sometimes working all night. One would have thought that establishing a chain of very popular off-the-peg menswear stores all over Australia, as well as personally running the manufacturing establishments to fill them, would have been enough. Now he was planning on branching out into designer clothes as well.

Deirdre suppressed a sigh. It was so difficult to tell Alan anything. He'd taken over as head of the family when he was only twenty, his father's unexpected death from a heart attack having left the family's clothes factory on the brink of receivership. Their home too had been found to be holding a second mortgage. Alan had had to work his fingers to the bone to pull them out of bankruptcy. But he'd succeeded, and succeeded very well. She was extremely proud of him.

The one unfortunate result of his success, however, was that he'd become rather bossy. He expected people just to go along with whatever he wanted. It must have come as a considerable shock, Deirdre realised, when the one woman who'd managed to capture his heart had upped and married another man a few years back.

Her head lifted, eyes narrowing with suspicion as she watched her son forking his *fettuccine marinara* into his mouth. 'Is Adrianna going to be there?' she asked casually.

His shrug seemed non-committal, but he was a master at hiding his feelings. 'I doubt it. Her label hasn't been entered into the competitions. She rarely comes to Sydney any more.' He lifted his dark, glossy head, his very male but rather cruel mouth curving back into a wry smile. 'Stop fishing, Mother. The reason I don't want to attend tonight is because I'm tired.'

'Then don't go. Stay home here and watch it on television with your poor old mum.'

He laughed, and Deirdre wished he would laugh more often. Laughter lent some warmth to his coldly handsome face, and those hard blue eyes of his.

'Poor old Mum, my foot. You're not poor. *I've* made sure of that! And secondly, at fifty-five, you're not old either. Why don't you do me and yourself a favour and find some nice man to occupy your time? Then I won't have to put up with your trying to organise *my* leisure time for me.'

'Do you *have* any leisure time?' she remarked archly.

'Occasionally.'

'Heaven knows when. Or what you do with it.'

Alan's laugh was dry. 'Don't you worry about what I do with my time, Mother. I'm a big boy now.'

But Deirdre *did* worry about him. Since Adrianna's rejection, Alan had not brought one woman home. She didn't for one moment imagine her handsome son was celibate, but she shuddered to think he might be indulging in one-night stands rather than risk being hurt again. She did so want him to get married and have children, but she dared not broach the subject. He was very prickly about his private life.

'Will Ebony be one of the models tonight, do you know?' she asked instead.

'I dare say,' Alan returned in that same flat tone he always used when the subject of Ebony came up these days. Deirdre knew her son well enough to know that when he sounded his most calm he was, in fact, at his most annoyed.

It was a wicked shame, she thought, that their once close relationship had been ruined by money. Ebony was a sweet girl, but too proud in Deirdre's opinion. Fancy taking offence when she found out that her parents' estate had been negligible, and that Alan—as her appointed guardian—had generously, but quite rightly, paid for all her education and expenses. What had she expected him to do? She'd only been fifteen, after all.

Still, when the girl had discovered shortly after leaving boarding-school at eighteen that this was so, she'd apparently been most upset. She and Alan had had some kind of altercation in the library over the situation, resulting in Ebony running to her room, crying. Deirdre had been unable to comfort her, the girl saying over and over that she had to leave.

At the time Ebony had been doing a grooming and modelling course that Deirdre herself had given her as a Christmas present that year. When the lady running the modelling course had recommended Ebony to a modelling agency, saying she had the potential to reach the top in that profession, the stubborn child had immediately dropped her idea of going to teacher-training college and had pursued a career that would start paying immediately.

She'd been an instant hit, on both the catwalk and behind the photographers' lenses, and it hadn't been long before she was giving Alan a cheque every week in repayment. Then, as soon as she'd been earning enough money, she had moved out of the house and into a flat of her own.

Alan had been furious, and had refused to speak of Ebony for a long long time. It wasn't till Deirdre had thrown her a twenty-first birthday party a little over a year ago that he had even deigned to be in the same room with her. Whenever she'd come to visit Deirdre on previous occasions, and Alan had been home, he would make some excuse to leave the house. This time, however, under threat from his mother, he had been civil to Ebony in front of the other guests, though far from pleased when he'd found out she was to stay the night. Forgiveness was not one of Alan's strong points.

The tension at the breakfast-table the following morning had been so acute that Deirdre had vowed never to ask Ebony to stay over again. It just wasn't worth it. But the ongoing feud was a thorn in her side. She loved the girl, thought of her as fondly as her own daughter, Vicki. Nothing would please her more than if her son and his ward made up.

'Don't you think it's time you and Ebony buried the hatchet?' she said with an unhappy sigh.

'I hardly think that's ever likely.'

'Why not? Maybe if you were *nicer* to her when you saw her, which you must do occasionally. You're in the same business.'

Alan's laugh was harsh. 'If I were *nice* to Ebony, she'd spit in my face.'

'Alan! She would not. Ebony's a lady.'

'Is she, now? Funny, I've never thought of her as such. A black-hearted witch, perhaps. But never a lady.'

Deirdre was truly shocked. 'Are we talking about the same girl here?'

'Oh, yes, Mother, we most certainly are. Your sweet Ebony has just never chosen to show you that side of herself.'

'I think you're biased.'

'Aye, that I am,' he agreed drily.

'What did you say to her that night in the library that upset her so much? I never could get the details of your argument out of her.'

Alan put down his serviette and rose. 'For pity's sake, Mother, that was nearly four years ago. How could I possibly remember? Probably told her she was an ungrateful little wretch, which she was. Now I must go. I have appointments lined up all afternoon with prospective designers dying to head my new Man-About-Town exclusive label.'

Walking round to peck her on the forehead, he strode from the patio into the living-room and towards the front door, an elegant figure in one of his own-brand business suits. Being six feet three and finely proportioned, Alan could have modelled his own products if he'd chosen to.

Deirdre watched him go with increasing unease. He was not happy, she decided, and, like all mothers, she wanted her son to be happy. She wanted both her children to be happy. Vicki seemed happy, living in a run-down house in Paddington with some artist whom she claimed to be mad about.

But he was the latest of a series of men she'd been 'mad about' during the past ten years. Anti-marriage and anti-establishment, Vicki had moved out of home when she was nineteen 'in search of her own identity', whatever that meant. Still, it was Vicki's life and she was supposed to be doing quite well, managing a record shop in Oxford Street, though she often dropped home to ask Alan for a 'loan', which he usually gave her along with a lecture.

Deirdre suspected, however, that Alan didn't mind giving his sister money—and advice—every now and then. He liked being needed. And he liked helping people.

'Mr Alan gone, has he?'

Deirdre sighed. 'Yes, Bob.'

He tut-tutted. 'That man works too hard. Have you finished too, Mrs Carstairs? Will I clear away?'

'Yes, do. It was lovely, Bob. You cook Italian like an Italian.'

The little man beamed, and began clearing the table, stacking up the plates with a very steady hand for a man pushing sixty. Deirdre watched him bustle off back into the kitchen, thinking to herself that he was another example of Alan's basic kindness.

Bob, and his twin brother, Bill, had up till two years ago lived on a chicken farm, with Bob tending to the household chores while Bill did the manual labour outside. Neither twin had ever married, both being very shy men. Their farm had been their life till the recession and high interest rates had sent them broke. Alan had spotted them being interviewed on a television programme on the day the bank was to repossess their property and evict them. Both men had broken down during the painful interview. It had torn Deirdre's heart out, making her cry.

When Alan had abruptly left the family room, she'd thought maybe he was upset too. And he probably had been. But, being a man of action, he'd left the room to telephone the station and start making arrangements to meet the elderly twin brothers. The upshot was Bob and Bill were brought to Sydney and installed in the Carstairses' home,

Bob as cook and cleaner, Bill as gardener and handyman. Alan had even had the old servants' quarters fitted out as a self-contained flat for them. Both men thought him a prince of the first order, and were devoted to his service. When Alan had casually mentioned one day that he liked Italian food, Bob had raced out and bought several Italian cookbooks with his own money.

Yes, Alan could do good deeds, but that didn't mean he wasn't a difficult man. Deirdre hoped he'd be polite to Ebony at the show tonight. Fancy his calling her a black-hearted witch! Why, Ebony was no such thing! She had always been such a sweet girl, pleasant and polite to her elders. She was a little aloof at times, but that was to be expected, given her background. Deirdre could not understand why Alan was so hard on her...

Ebony came out on to the catwalk, tall and sophisticated in a black wool dress that was basically strapless but had a black lace overlay that went right up to the neck and down her arms in tight sleeves. If the intention of the lace was modesty, then it failed miserably.

Every male in the room snapped to attention as she moved with a lithe, sensuous grace down that raised pathway, her waist-length straight black hair draped over one shoulder and her deeply set black eyes projecting a dark, mysterious allure from underneath black, winged brows. Her wide, full mouth was painted a deep scarlet in vivid contrast to her white, white skin.

Alan shifted uncomfortably in his chair and looked away. He needed no reminders of what she looked like, or how easily she could bewitch.

'Geez, Alan,' the man seated next to him whispered. 'And to think you had *that* living under your roof all those years. How did you stand it, man?'

'Familiarity breeds contempt, my friend,' he returned smoothly. 'Besides, she doesn't look the same without her make-up on.'

'I'd like an opportunity to wake up in bed with her one morning and judge that for myself,' came the dry rejoinder. 'Still, from what I've heard, I'm not her type.'

Alan straightened in his chair. 'Oh? And what's her type?'

'Photographers, I gather.'

'Meaning?'

'God, Alan, don't you know anything about your own ward's life. Our supermodel is reported to have had a fling with all of her photographers so far. She and Gary Stevenson were a really hot item a couple of years ago before he took off for Paris. But he's back in Sydney now and has clearly taken up where he left off. I saw them myself only today, having lunch down at a café in Darling Harbour.'

'Is that so?'

'You don't sound concerned. Stevenson's a good deal older than her, you know.'

Alan tried not to bristle, but did, anyway. 'He's only in his thirties.'

'Closer to forty. And how old's your Ebony?'

'Twenty-two. And she's *not* my Ebony,' he bit out. 'She's a free agent. Now, can we watch the show? We've paid two hundred dollars a seat for this ringside table. Let's get our money's worth.'

Alan's colleague settled back in a disgruntled silence, leaving Alan forced to pretend to watch the rest of the parade. Ebony had been up and down a couple of times by now, and was sashaying back towards the group of models who were waiting their turn in front of the huge red velvet curtain. The highly sensual sway of her curvaceous buttocks and hips sent a cold fury into his veins.

Does she know what she's doing? he wondered savagely. Does she know I'm here?

Of course she does, came the bitter answer. She's a witch, a black-hearted witch!

God damn you to hell, Ebony Theroux.

He parked in the street opposite the three-storey square building that housed her flat, watching and waiting for her to come home. What he would do if she showed up with Stevenson, or any of her other numerous admirers, God only knew. Would he be able to meekly drive on? Or would he find some way to spoil her night, as she had already spoiled his?

He'd vowed after the last argument they'd had not to have anything further to do with her, *never* to come here to see her again. But he'd vowed that the time before as well.

His teeth clenched down hard in his jaw, his stomach muscles tightening. Would he never rid himself of this gut-wrenching desire? It had been four years now. Four painful, soul-destroying years. He really could not allow it to go on. He would have to do something about it.

But he'd said that before, as well.

A light snapped on in her flat, sending a wave of near-nausea churning through his innards. He hadn't seen her enter the building, anger at this crazy but uncontrollable desire having distracted him for a moment. Now, she'd slipped in without his knowing if she was alone or not.

He stared up at the square of light, his eyes darting left as he waited anxiously for her bedroom light to be switched on as well. That was a large window with gauzy curtains. If she had someone with her, he would soon know.

The light remained off.

After several tortuous minutes, he couldn't stand the waiting any longer. With an agitated, jerky movement, he extracted the keys from the ignition, not bothering to put the steering lock on, only just remembering to lock the door before swinging it shut. It was only when the bitter winter air cut through him that he remembered his overcoat draped over the passenger seat.

'Damn it!' he swore, and, ramming his keys and hands into the trouser pockets of his black dinner suit, strode angrily across the dimly lit street and up to the locked security door. For a moment he hesitated, self-disgust urging him to turn right round and go home. But other forces were at work, forces far stronger than pride. He jabbed the buzzer on flat eight with his finger.

His heart began to thud, disgusting him further. Why did he let her do this to him? Why?

'Yes?' came the low, husky query that sent a shiver down his hunched spine.

'It's Alan,' he said, despising himself.

'Alan . . .' she repeated as though trying to recall whom she might know called Alan.

He bit his tongue to stop himself from snapping at her. Male ego demanded he play her at her own game, keeping his cool, not allowing her any more triumph than was strictly necessary.

'What do you want, Alan?'

To strangle you, he thought viciously. God, but she liked turning the screw.

'For pity's sake, Ebony, it's bitter out here. Just let me in. Or aren't you alone?' he finished cuttingly.

There was a moment's tense silence from the intercom before a buzzing sound indicated she had opened the door. Alan hated himself for the rush of relief, not to mention the rush of something else that immediately stampeded through his body. But already he was on that treadmill of excitement that she could generate without any conscious effort. He couldn't look at her these days without wanting her so badly that it was a painful ache in his loins.

She met him at the door, still wearing that damned black dress. It was one of her contract conditions, that whenever she did a fashion parade she kept the clothes she modelled. The designers didn't mind. The fabulous Ebony wearing their clothes in public was great advertising, and cheaper than most.

'That dress looks even better up close,' he said in a desire-thickened voice.

She eyed him coolly over the rim of a glass of white wine, sipping while those black eyes stripped his soul naked. 'So you *were* there tonight,' she remarked casually, and, turning, began walking across the tiled foyer and into the living-room. Alan was left to come in alone and close the door behind him, following her as she wandered, glass in hand, into her strikingly furnished flat.

Alan glanced around the lounge-room and marvelled at the effect she had achieved with just a few pieces of furniture. Had she deliberately chosen white as a foil for her colouring, or in cold mockery of what white usually represented? He wouldn't put it past her. He wouldn't put anything past her.

She kicked off her shoes and curled herself into one of the squashy white leather sofas that flanked the mock-fireplace. A gas fire was softly burning, highlighting the blue-black sheen on that gorgeous hair as well as sending a warm honey glow to her complexion. She must have washed off some of that stark white make-up, he thought as his hot gaze travelled down her body and up again. Her mouth was still red, though. Red and softly pouting.

Alan swallowed.

Once settled, she threw an indifferent glance at him over her shoulder. 'Pour yourself some wine,' she suggested, and waved a scarlet-nailed hand towards the kitchen. 'The bottle's in the fridge.'

'No, thanks,' he said stiffly, hating her for the way she always made him feel so darned awkward.

She said not a word while she drank the rest of her wine, placing the empty glass down on the marble coffee-table with a small, shuddering sigh. 'Must you stand there like that with your hands in your pockets?' she said. 'You make me uncomfortable.'

His harsh laughter drew her eyes. 'Do I indeed? That's only fair, then.'

'Fair?' Those exquisitely shaped eyebrows lifted. 'What's that supposed to mean?'

'Nothing,' he muttered, and began walking slowly towards her. For a second he could have sworn he saw fear on her face. But just as swiftly, her expression changed to one of cool composure.

'I have my final cheque ready to give you. I'll get it.' She was up and past him before he could do more than breathe her perfume. Still, as the exotic scent teased his nostrils, he felt his loins prickle in instant response. It angered him.

'I did not come here for a cheque, Ebony. You know damned well I never wanted you to pay me back in the first place.'

Her smile was wry as she produced the cheque from a drawer. 'Ah, yes, Alan, but what *you* want does not always have priority in my life.'

'Meaning?'

Her eyes were like black coals, and just as hard. 'Meaning I want you to take this cheque and get the hell out of my life. I don't ever want to see you again. I'm going to be married.'

'Married!' Something exploded in Alan's head. She couldn't be getting married. He wouldn't let her. She was *his*!

'That's right,' she went on brusquely. 'To Gary Stevenson. He asked me today. He wants me to go back to Paris with him, and I'm going to.'

'I don't believe you.'

'Then I suggest you do, Alan. It's over between us. Over!'

'Is it, by God? I don't think so, Ebony. Not at all.' Snatching the cheque out of her hands, he ripped it into shreds before pulling her into his arms and kissing her till both of them were gasping for breath.

When she spun out of his grasp he caught her and yanked her back against him, one hand pressing her stomach so that her buttocks were hard against his arousal, the other wrapped around her heaving breasts. 'I won't let you go,' he rasped, his panting mouth against her ear. 'You're mine, Ebony. *Mine*!'

In a wild desperation, he started kissing her neck and stroking her braless breasts through the dress, the blood roaring through his veins as he felt the nipples harden beneath his hands. When he finally heard her groan, elation swept through him, steeling his sense of purpose, and his determination to win her total surrender one more time. Tomorrow did not figure largely in his mind. Nor the future. Not even her threatened marriage.

All he knew was that he had to have her naked beneath him, have her tremble as only she could tremble, have her take him to those places no other woman had ever taken him before.

'Alan, no,' she groaned again.

But it sounded like a yes to his impassioned ears. He had no mercy for her protests or her tears. He kept up the kissing and the touching till she gave one last shudder and whirled in his arms. Only then could he perhaps have seen the despair in her eyes, if he'd been capable of seeing *anything* beyond his own excruciating need. As it was, all he saw was that ripe red mouth, soft and swollen and seductive. He wanted to lose himself in that mouth, to have those pouting lips kiss him all over, to have them tease and torment his flesh till he could stand it no longer.

So that when she swept her arms up around his neck and pulled his mouth down to hers in a kiss far more brutal than any she'd ever sought before, his only thoughts were of what awaited him behind her bedroom door.

'I hate you,' she choked out when he scooped her up into his arms and carried her into that bedroom.

His blue eyes glittered in the semi-darkness. 'I love the way you hate, Ebony. Keep it up.' And with that, he dropped her on the bed and started stripping off her clothes.

CHAPTER TWO

EBONY woke the next morning knowing that she finally hated Alan Carstairs.

It had been a long time coming.

At fifteen, she had hero-worshipped him. At sixteen, she'd developed a full-blown schoolgirl crush. By seventeen, she was constantly fantasising about him, till finally, at eighteen, she'd made an utter fool of herself over the man.

She cringed at the still sharp memory of her throwing herself at him in the library that night four years ago, gushing with adolescent stupidity that he must love her if he'd paid for her out of his own pocket all these years. He hadn't known what had hit him when she'd upped and kissed him. How ironic that it had probably been his momentary but stunning response to that foolish kiss that had been responsible for what had happened three years later.

Oh, he'd stopped the kiss soon enough, well before he could have been accused of tampering with her morals. But the memory of his tongue thrusting deep into her mouth, of his arms tightening like steel bands around her even for a split-second, had been enough to keep fuelling her fantasy that underneath his bluster he loved her and wanted her.

And she'd naïvely told him so.

Of course, he'd torn strips off her at the time, telling her she was acting like a silly little fool, that his paying for her had been his way of showing gratitude to her father who'd once lent him money when no one else would, that he considered her guardianship a sacred trust that could not and would not be sullied by him, that his briefly kissing her back had been meant as a savage lesson on what could happen if a hormone-filled teenager like herself fell into the wrong hands.

She'd finally believed him that night, shame and embarrassment making her flee his presence. How she had cried and cried! Nothing Mrs Carstairs said—and the dear woman had tried everything— could make her stop. All Ebony had been able to think of was that she couldn't stay in that house, seeing Alan every day, reliving her moment of humiliation, living off his charity. She had seized on this last reason as an excuse to flee him, and his house, as soon as she could.

But she hadn't been able to forget him, no matter what she'd done. Hard work and a busy and varied social life had filled her hours, but not her heart.

Gary Stevenson had come into her life when she'd been a very vulnerable twenty. Still a virgin, despite her physical beauty attracting many admirers, Gary had become first her photographer, then her friend, and finally her lover.

Why had she given in to him and not the others?

He'd been good to her. Sweet. Kind. And one night he had caught her at a very weak moment. Afterwards, there had seemed to be no going back.

And in truth, she'd found much comfort in the human closeness of their affair, in having Gary hold her and tell her that he adored the ground she walked on. Oh, he hadn't pretended to really love her, which had been a relief in a way. His being in love with her might have made her feel guilty. But he'd liked her and desired her and, in the end, had even asked her to marry him. They would go to Paris together, he'd said, and become a raging success.

She had had to refuse, of course, and, though disappointed, Gary had not been heart-broken, taking himself off to Paris anyway while she had gone on with her modelling here in Sydney. For a while, she'd been very depressed and lonely, thinking she'd done the wrong thing. But then the unexpected had happened. Alan had become her lover, and she'd quickly found that what she'd experienced in bed with Gary had not prepared her for the intoxicating excitement and wickedly irresistible rapture of being in Alan's arms.

Which is why I'm here now, she groaned silently, and threw a pained look across at Alan's sleeping form.

God, why do I let him do this to me—take my self-respect and pride and grind it into the dust, make me say and do things when I know he doesn't love me? He told me the morning after the first night I slept with him. He loves Adrianna. What he feels for me is nothing but lust, an uncontrollably mad lust.

Ebony could still recall the horror she'd felt when he'd told her that, and then added that he wanted to keep their relationship a secret from the world, and especially his mother. Their passion for each other would pass, he'd claimed. No need to hurt anybody with the knowledge of their liaison when it was only a fleeting thing.

Yet all the while he'd been saying this, *she* had been hurting. More than hurting—breaking into little pieces. She'd argued with him on this last score, wanting him at least to recognise in public that she was his woman. But no... People would not understand, he'd said. They'd talk.

So he'd kept her as a hole-and-corner mistress, to be visited in the dead of night, to be used for his pleasure in private while the world at large saw them as almost enemies.

And she had gone along with it, despising herself while counting the days till he came to her again, then vainly trying to salvage some pride by never showing any affection or special consideration towards him, by reducing his visits to nothing more than raw sexual encounters, with no love or warmth involved. There was a perverse pleasure in taunting him with her cold indifference to whether he came or not, in letting him think that there were plenty of other fish in the sea to fill her empty bed if he wasn't in it, in feeding his crazed jealousies that she might actually do some of the things she did with him with other lovers.

As if she would. Not even Gary had been able to coax such intimacies from her, or such abandonment. Only Alan...

Tears filled Ebony's eyes, but she dashed them away with the backs of her hands. The time for tears was long gone. Now it was time for action.

Last night had proved beyond the shadow of a doubt that she had no strength against Alan's sexual power over her. No matter how angry with him she was, he only had to touch her and she was lost.

And it would always be that way, she agonised. Love him or hate him, she was his for the taking whenever he wanted her. It was this mortifying re-alisation that propelled her not to change her mind from what she had already decided she must do— go to Paris with Gary.

Shivering a little, she slipped out of the warmth of the bed and dragged on her white bathrobe over her naked and vaguely aching body. She flushed guiltily to think it had been herself—and not Alan— who had been the insatiable one last night. Was it because she had known this would be the last time?

Probably. Even now, the temptation to return to that bed, to rouse him from sleep with her hands and lips, to...

A bitter taste filled her mouth. Maybe it was just that she needed to clean her teeth, or maybe it was the self-hate rising from within. Whatever, she suddenly felt unclean, wicked, rotten to the core. She had to get away from him, from Sydney, from Australia. That was the only answer.

Slipping quietly out into the lounge-room, she picked up her telephone and dialled the number she'd written on the notebook resting beside it.

'The Ramada,' the hotel receptionist answered.

'Could you put me through to Gary Stevenson's room, please?'

'Certainly, madam.'

Ebony's eyes flicked anxiously over at the bedroom door while waiting for Gary to answer. She hoped Alan wouldn't wake up. Instinct warned her she must keep her plans a secret. Alan must never find out, not till she was safely on that plane.

A bleary-voiced Gary finally came on the line. 'Hello.'

'It's Ebony,' she said quickly, huskily. 'I need to see you. This morning. Will you be in around nine?'

'Sure thing, love. What's the urgency? You've already turned me down. Again.'

'I've had second thoughts. Sort of.'

'Only "sort of"?'

'We need to talk.'

'I'm all ears.'

'Not on the phone.'

'Why not?'

She hesitated, then said softly, 'I'm not alone.'

Gary's chuckle was dark. 'So that's the way it is, eh? What's the problem? Won't he take the hint he's no longer wanted?'

'Something like that.'

'I see . . .' His sigh was weary. 'Well, get rid of him temporarily, love, and get over here pronto. If you feel as bad as you sound, then methinks you need a shoulder to cry on.'

A lump filled her throat. 'You're so good to me, Gary.'

'Yeah, yeah, all my exes say that. I'm a good bloke. But tell me one thing. How come in the movies—and I suspect in life—it's always the bad guy who ends up with the girl? Oh, never mind. I'll be here when you get here, love. See you.' And he hung up.

Ebony lowered the receiver silently back into its cradle, but, when she turned, there was Alan, standing in the open doorway, thunder on his face.

'You *can't* marry Stevenson,' he ground out. 'You don't love him.'

She glared at him, standing there in the nude, as arrogant as you please. And as lethally attractive. Not an ounce of fat graced his tall, lean body, a light covering of dark hair giving him a primitive appeal. Put a spear in his hand and he would make a good savage, she thought bitterly.

'How do you know?' she said, using her fingers to comb her tangled hair back from her face till it fell into a sleek black curtain down her back.

'Because you're incapable of loving any man,' he stated harshly.

Her short bark of laughter was half disbelief, half mocking. 'Certainly not a man like you!'

His blue eyes blazed for a second before adopting an expression of cold contempt. 'Then why keep going to bed with me?'

She shrugged. 'Perhaps I'm a masochist.'

'A hedonist, perhaps, not a masochist. You enjoy pleasure, Ebony, not pain. And you can't deny I give you pleasure.'

'I wouldn't dream of denying it.'

When she moved to brush past him on the way to the bathroom, his hand shot out to enclose her upper arm in a vice-like grip. 'You can't go from me to Stevenson,' he rasped.

She locked eyes with him, aware of nothing but the emotional quaver in his voice. Could that be love talking? she puzzled briefly before dismissing such a stupid notion. No. Not love. Possessiveness. Jealousy. Male ego. But not love. Alan's heart already belonged elsewhere. If he had a heart, that was. She was beginning to doubt it.

'I have to talk to him,' she admitted, then added, 'I have to tell him personally that I'm not going to marry him.'

There was no way she could have mistaken the relief in Alan's eyes. But that didn't prove anything, except he wasn't ready yet to give up his private supply of free sex. Free in every way. Emotionally, financially and physically. What man would want to give up such a cushy arrangement?

When he went to draw her back into his arms, she yanked out of his grasp and took a step backwards. 'No,' she said coldly. 'I have to shower and dress. Then I'm leaving.'

'What happened to breakfast?'

'I'm not having any. If you want some, get it yourself.'

His smile was sardonic. 'So kind of you.'

'Oh, but I'm not kind, Alan. There again, you don't want me for my kindness, do you?'

'Hardly.'

'Then don't complain. You've got your way. I'm not marrying Gary. What more do you want from me?'

'Not a thing,' he bit out.

'Then if you'll excuse me?'

He watched her sweep into the bathroom, black anger in his heart. What more did he want of her? He wanted her to grovel at his feet, to beg him to visit her more often, to suffer from the same type of blind, obsessive need that was even now sending the blood pounding through his veins, making his flesh expand into a tight, painful instrument of torture.

Only an instinct that seducing Ebony this morning might rebound on him in some way made him put that solution to his frustration aside. All he could do was wait for her to leave and then he would plunge his pained body beneath the coldest of showers till he could comfortably face the day ahead.

Meanwhile he would dive back under the bed-covers and pass the time contemplating the many and varied ways he could exact vengeance on this creature who had been tying him in knots for years.

Yes, years!

Four, to be exact. He couldn't count the first three. She'd spent most of them in boarding-school. And while at fifteen she'd been a budding beauty, her shy, almost introverted nature at that time had protected her from male admiration, his own included.

Not that he would have dreamt of seeing Pierre's daughter in that light, especially at such a tender age. No, he was not guilty of that, thank God. Still, he remembered having enjoyed her company when he'd taken her on the occasional outing back then, finding her opinions surprisingly mature and her gestures of gratitude towards him quite touching. He actually still kept a pair of gold cuff-links she'd given him for his twenty-eighth birthday, after saving the money herself from delivering pamphlets during the school holidays.

Where had that sweet child gone to? he wondered. When had she turned from virgin to vamp?

A type of guilt twisted his heart. Surely it couldn't have been *his* fault, could it? That night, in the library... She'd caught him unawares, kissing him like that. For a few seconds he'd completely lost control. Hell, he could still recall how it had felt as her soft, breathless mouth had flowered eagerly open to accept the thrust of his tongue, as well as the way her heart had beat madly against his.

For a split-second, he'd wanted to forget his conscience and just drown in her delicious young body. He'd been tempted to take it for his pleasure and his pleasure alone, knowing he could seduce her virginal flesh quite easily, knowing he could mould and form her, body and soul, to his wants and needs.

She wouldn't have stopped him. He knew it. So in the end he had had to stop himself. He'd thought himself so right, so noble, so... good. He'd been made her guardian, for God's sake, not her corrupter. Not even her teenage declaration of undying love had swayed his determination to put aside such a wicked temptation. Not then, nor during the subsequent years as she'd gone from child to woman, from a shy and somewhat awkward teenager to a sophisticated and successful model, had he wavered in his resolve.

The crunch had come, predictably enough, at her twenty-first birthday party. He should have known seeing her on that occasion would be his undoing. It had been three years before, on her eighteenth birthday, that his lust had first raised its ugly head. Till then, he'd only ever seen Ebony in either her school uniform or shapeless jeans and tops. Teenage girls never seemed to wear anything else.

But that fateful night, his mother had bought her a white lace dress that might have been virginal on the peg. On eighteen-year-old Ebony, complete with make-up and high heels, it looked so seductive that it was criminal. When Alan had spotted her coming down the stairs, his heart had stopped beating. Not so the rest of his body. It had leapt with a desire so fierce and so instant that he'd been thunderstruck.

He'd stared at Ebony and she had stared right back, those deep black eyes of hers showing not a hint of understanding of what was happening to him. *Had* she understood? Was that why she'd been so shocked that evening in the library a few months later when he'd knocked her back, scorned her offer of love?

Maybe. Maybe not.

Ebony's thoughts and motives were a mystery to him. *She* was a mystery. Sometimes he wondered if those three years of sacrifice had all been a wicked waste. Maybe at eighteen she'd already started on her sexual journey; maybe she hadn't been a virgin at all.

She certainly hadn't been a virgin three years later. And how!

There was no peace for his flesh as he recalled what Ebony had done to him the night of her twenty-first birthday. No peace at all.

She'd been a bit tipsy, of course, and the guests had left. But that was no excuse for stripping off all her clothes and blatantly going swimming in the pool in the nude in full view of him. She'd claimed afterwards she hadn't known he was there, but he didn't believe her. She'd been watching out for him all night, baiting him, tempting him.

Besides, there'd been no resistance whatsoever when she'd climbed out of the water and he'd come forward to draw her dripping nakedness against him, nor when he'd claimed her supposedly startled mouth in a hungry kiss. She'd been more than willing to let him touch her all over, to take her right there by the pool, to carry her back to his room where he'd worked his will upon her body all night.

Naturally, he *had* heard the rumours about her, but rumours about models were rife and not always true. For some inexplicable reason, he'd been reluctant to believe she could be as promiscuous as people said she was. He had found out that night that she was all that and more. Never had he known a woman so wild and wanton and willing. She was sex mad, he decided. Totally sex mad. Just like her father.

His first thought the next morning had been that he had to keep what had happened from his mother, as he'd kept from her the rumours about Ebony's private life. His mother thought Ebony a sweet, old-fashioned girl and he didn't want to destroy that illusion, or the close relationship the two women enjoyed.

Maybe he had explained it badly to the naked girl in his arms. He hadn't meant to hurt her, though he suspected he had. But what was to be gained by dressing up reality with false words of love? It wasn't as though she were an innocent, whose sensitive feelings had to be treated with kid gloves.

They lusted after each other. That was the plain and unvarnished truth. In a way, it was fortuitous that Ebony was of such a highly sexed nature, since not many women would have endured the kind of unrestrained lovemaking he'd insisted upon in an effort to rid himself of his own insatiable need. With a bit of luck, he might not need any repeat performance.

Or so he had deluded himself at the time.

Alan made a scoffing sound just as Ebony came out of the bathroom, made-up but not dressed. She was breathtakingly nude, the exquisiteness of her beauty stabbing at his heart. And elsewhere.

God, but Mother Nature had been cruel, sending a creature like her to torment him. Or was it the devil himself who had fashioned that incredible face and body? Yes, that sounded right. Who but Satan would be wicked enough to combine all those assets, to give one woman everything that a man could possibly want? Long, silken black hair that screamed out to be stroked; exotic, thickly lashed ebony eyes that flashed fire and promised pleasure at the same time; a full-lipped smouldering mouth which would tempt a saint. And that was only her face.

Her body was another dimension, another hell to be endured. High, pointy breasts with large pink areolae and long, sensitive nipples, a delightfully tiny waist, deliciously curvaceous hips and long, long legs that wound their shapely way down to dainty ankles and feet.

Then there was her skin . . .

What man wouldn't want to run his hands over her skin, the pale magnolia-like skin whose texture was like cool velvet, till it was heated by desire. Then it would glow. It was glowing now. But not with passion. With the heat of the shower. Her eyes were cold as they raked over him.

'You still here?' she said scathingly.

He gnashed his teeth as she went about dressing in front of him, first drawing on a silk black teddy, then sliding into a black woollen jumpsuit.

Black was Ebony's trademark. She wore nothing else, modelled nothing else. So was her lack of smiling, her full lips looking far better fashioned into a sullen, sulky or seductive pout.

Alan would have thought that such restrictions would have been disastrous to her career, but, surprisingly, it had all worked in her favour, creating an individual and highly sensual image that kept her and her agency busy.

'I have to go, Alan,' she said briskly, popping on black pumps before picking up a black holdall and heading for the bedroom door. Only then did she stop for an indifferent look at him over her shoulder. 'Lock up when you leave, will you? And wash up any mess you make.'

One day, Alan thought as he lay there, fuming. One day he was going to wipe that cool composure from that beautiful face of hers. One day he was going to make her cry. And what would he do? Walk away. That was what he'd do.

Oh, sure, sure, came a dark, cynical voice.

Flinging back the sheet, Alan leapt from the bed and marched into the bathroom where he snapped on the cold water jets. Bracing himself, he stepped under the freezing cold spray, telling himself it was penance for his sins.

He must have had a lot of sins on his soul, for he had to stay in the shower for a long, long time.

CHAPTER THREE

EBONY slumped into the back seat of the taxi, strain telling on her face. The façade she always put on in a vain attempt to punish Alan was beginning to take its toll. How long before she actually became that person for real? Brittle and cynical and cruel.

It was the cruel part that bothered her the most.

There was no doubt about it. She had to get out from under the crippling effects of this appalling affair before she self-destructed.

Sighing, Ebony closed her eyes, her head tipping back against the seat. It wasn't far from her flat in Randwick to the Ramada Hotel, but at eight-thirty in the morning she was in for at least half an hour's run into the city. Might as well try to rest.

Rest was not on the agenda for her troubled soul that morning, however. She was too full of regrets and bitter recriminations, the main one being why she had allowed Alan to become her lover in the first place. There'd been no seduction, no courtship, no nothing. All he'd done was look at her a few times on the night of her twenty-first birthday party.

But that was all it had taken to start her heart beating madly for him, not to mention make her grasp at straws where his feelings were concerned, especially when once or twice she had surprised him staring at her with desire in his eyes. Had he too not forgotten that kiss in the library three years before? she'd begun wondering. Could he have been lying that night, saying he didn't really want her when all along he had?

It would be the sort of gallant thing Alan might do, she'd reasoned, considering his over-active sense of responsibility towards those under his care. He was very protective of all the females in his family, including his mother and that wayward sister of his. Maybe he'd believed that, at eighteen, Ebony was too young for him, far too young to embark on the kind of relationship he might want and need; certainly far too young for marriage.

That possibility had tormented her for the rest of the party, sparking a resolve to confront Alan later that night. She'd long given up any hope of getting the man out of her system, so, if there was a chance that some twisted scruple was keeping them apart, then she'd aimed to try to unravel it. Who knew? Maybe her turning twenty-one had already heralded a change in his attitude towards her. Maybe he was now beginning to think of her as a grown woman, an adult, not the child who'd come into his home as a young and innocent fifteen-year-old.

This train of thought had excited her. Why hadn't she reasoned this all out before? Of course that was it! His sexual response three years ago had made him feel guilty. But there was no longer any need for guilt. Couldn't he see that? She couldn't wait to talk to him alone, to tell him that time had not changed what *she* felt for *him*, but that time *had* changed the status quo between them. He was no longer her guardian in any way. He was simply a man, as she was a woman.

But when she had turned round from seeing the last guest leave shortly after one-thirty, it had been to find Alan saying an abrupt goodnight and striding off to bed. Frustrated at having her wishes thwarted, Ebony had wandered around the house for ages, helping clean up, afterwards sitting alone in the kitchen, finishing off one of the half-empty bottles of champagne, thinking it might help her sleep.

No such luck. It had fizzed through her veins, sparking further restlessness. Having swallowed the last drop of wine, she had walked out on to the back patio and down the steps to the next terrace where she had stood and stared, first out across the darkened harbour waters, then down at the heated pool.

A swim will tire me out, she'd decided, make me sleep...

Positive she was alone, Ebony had slipped the tiny straps of her black crêpe party dress off her shoulders, shimmying till it had slid down over her hips and pooled on to the pebble-effect concrete. Stepping out of the circle, she had kicked off her shoes then peeled off her panties and tights.

The night air might have felt cool on her naked flesh, if her blood hadn't been so heated by the wine. She had balanced for a few moments on the edge of the pool before flicking her long sweep of hair back over her shoulders and diving into the water.

If she had known for a second that Alan had been sitting in the shadows of the pool-house, she would never have dreamt of being so provocative as to go skinny-dipping in front of him. She certainly wouldn't have floated up and down the pool on her back, idly splashing water over her breasts and stomach.

She'd really believed herself alone when she had climbed out of the water, and stood there, wringing her hair dry. Her shock when he had materialised out of the darkness had been very real. But he hadn't allowed her any opportunity to speak, or explain. He had simply swept her hard against him, uncaring if his clothes were ruined, uncaring of anything but his ruthless intention to reduce her to a trembling mass of unconditional surrender.

It hadn't been difficult. She'd been half aroused already from the way he'd looked at her earlier in the night. That, combined with her long-suppressed love just dying for expression, had made her a ready victim for his lust.

The trouble was she hadn't interpreted his actions as lust at the time. She'd mistakenly believed that he had finally realised his own love for her, had at last given in to an extremely powerful and very natural need to make love to her.

Ebony groaned silently at the memory of her very rapid capitulation.

How could she have been so naïve not to have seen there was nothing loving in the way he had kissed her and touched her? His hands had been quite rough on her flesh, demanding no quarter.

But by the time he'd pulled her over down on top of him on one of the deck-chairs, she'd been beside herself with passion and emotion. Alan loved her and desired her and needed her. There had been no question of not doing what he had clearly so desperately wanted.

Even now she could still recall the animal cry of satisfaction he had emitted when his body had finally fused with hers. Never mind that he hadn't waited to undress properly, or that someone could have come down from the house and caught them in the act. She had been making love to the man she loved and who loved her.

It was not till the morning after that she was forced to review her way of looking at their first coupling, then all their subsequent couplings during that long and tempestuous night. Not till Alan had made his appalling suggestion in his bed at dawn had Ebony seen that what she'd thought of as love on his part had been only lust, and that his 'making love' to her had been no more than 'having sex'.

She had hoped to become Alan's wife. Instead he'd offered her the role of his secret mistress. She hadn't been at all happy about it, but he'd secured her continued co-operation by turning up at her flat when least expected, then seducing her with a finesse that was as intoxicating as it was merciless.

For fourteen months, she'd endured his spasmodic visits, dying a little each time he came and left, hating herself for her weakness, yet unable to stop. More than once, she'd vowed to cut him dead, to send him away, unsatisfied. Whether he had sensed this or not, she couldn't be sure. But whenever she'd reached that point, he wouldn't come near her for weeks. Then he'd turn up out of the blue and, without saying a word, take her into his arms and start kissing her before she could utter a word of protest.

Those were the worst times—and the best—their lovemaking on the edge of violence, but so passionate and intense that she would despair afterwards of ever being able to give him up.

Could she now? Would she have the courage to take that step and walk away? No, *fly* away.

'Lady! We're here,' the taxi driver growled.

Ebony snapped to attention. Already the concierge at the Ramada was opening the car door for her. Checking the fare on the meter, she handed the driver a twenty-dollar note, told him to keep the change, then alighted with her usual style. Old habits died hard, and she was a model first, cool and composed and sophisticated. The shattered woman inside would remain hidden from everyone, even Gary. She was not about to tell him all the grim details of her relationship with Alan, only enough to make her plan feasible.

'Bob says you didn't come home last night.'

Alan took a sip of the black coffee his secretary had just brought in. 'Really, Mother,' he sighed into the phone, 'I'm not a child who has to answer for his actions. So I stayed out all night? So what? It's not the first time.'

'I realise that. That's what's bothering me. You're working too hard, Alan. Only yesterday you said how tired you were. Yet I'll guarantee you went from those awards to the office again. Or was it the factory this time?'

'Neither.'

'*Neither*? Then where, in heaven's name, did you get to?'

'Need I spell it out for you? I spent the night with a woman.' Something inside Alan twisted as he said that last word, yet he could not deny that Ebony would be a woman in everyone else's eyes. Though maybe not his mother's. God, but she'd be appalled if she knew whom he'd spent the night with.

'Oh,' was all she said, ever the tactful parent.

'No more questions?' Alan mocked.

'Would you tell me if I asked?'

'No.'

'So I won't. But I feel sorry for whoever she is.'

Alan bristled. 'What's that supposed to mean?'

'It means I hope she isn't in love with you, because you and I both know you're not in love with her. Or are you?'

Alan was startled, then annoyed. Ebony, in love with him? That was a laugh. As for himself... to even think about what he felt for her in terms of love was preposterous. Love was what his mother and father had shared, what Adrianna felt for Bryce McLean. Maybe even what Vicki felt for that excuse for a man she was living with. Love was not this black torture that wrung his soul every time he thought of Ebony, especially when he thought of what she might be getting up to when he wasn't around.

Had she lied to him about Stevenson this morning? he began worrying. Was she, at this very moment, in bed with her ex-lover? If she was, and he found out, he wasn't sure what he'd do, but it wouldn't be pleasant.

'I hate to disillusion you, Mother,' he bit out. 'But these days, women are as capable of staying the night with a man *without* love as vice versa.'

'My, my, you *are* out of sorts this morning. Maybe you're not as capable of staying the night with a woman without love as you think. But as you say, that's your private business. You don't have to answer to me. The reason I rang is because I'm worried about Ebony.'

Everything inside Alan tightened. 'Ebony?'

'Truly, Alan, you are the limit! Are you trying to pretend now you don't know who Ebony is?'

'I wish I didn't,' he muttered under his breath.

Deirdre Carstairs sighed. 'You saw her last night, didn't you?'

A few ghastly seconds passed before Alan realised his mother was talking about the fashion show, not later. 'Not to talk to,' he hedged.

'Did you think she looked all right? She seemed very pale and thin on television.'

'Ebony has always been pale and thin.'

'Well, she looked extra pale and thin to me. You don't think she's getting that dieting disease, do you?'

'Anorexia? No, I'm sure she isn't. Black always makes women look slimmer, Mother, as you very well know. And the make-up she wore was that stark white look. Ebony's just fine.' More than fine, he added in vicious silence, thinking of those long slender thighs wrapped around him, and those firm white breasts with their long pink nipples arching up towards his mouth.

He shuddered.

'I'm still worried,' his mother persisted. 'It's been ages since she came to see me and I know why. It's because of you, Alan. You and your rudeness. I won't stand for it any more, I tell you. I'm going to invite her over for dinner and you're going to be there. Not only are you going to be there, but you're going to be nice to her.'

'Mother, if Ebony knows I'm going to be there, she won't come.'

'Then we won't tell her, will we? We'll let her think you'll be away on business that night.'

Yes, Alan thought. There would be a certain sadistic pleasure in having her sitting at the table next to him, forced to be polite, unable to deliver any of those cutting little barbs of hers.

A malicious smile tugged at his lips. It would be an excellent revenge for that pathetic lie of hers that she was going to marry Gary Stevenson. For one ghastly moment, he'd thought she meant it, till he'd realised it was just another of those taunting, goading things she liked to say. It was another of her ploys to worry him, to make him jealous, to make him explode into the violent passion that turned her on so. Playing such games was part of her dark side, the side she kept hidden from everyone else.

Yes, he would enjoy making her squirm in front of his mother, enjoy it immensely.

'You're right, Mother,' he said expansively. 'Our feud has gone on long enough, but I do think we will have to surprise Ebony with my presence, otherwise she will find some excuse not to come.'

'I realise that, but I do so hate being deceitful...'

'Come, now,' he soothed. 'Your intentions are the best.' Even if mine aren't.

Deirdre brightened immediately. 'Yes, yes, they are. And if it means you two will become friends again, then it will be worth it. I'm so glad you're going to be co-operative, Alan. I'll call and ask her for tomorrow night. Friday.'

'Let's hope she's free.'

She was, as it turned out. But once the invitation had been accepted and the plan was in place, Alan was besieged with doubts. It was a dangerous thing to do, deceiving Ebony. The witch had a way of turning the tables on him.

Still, he could not deny that he was looking forward to seeing her again so soon, to feasting his eyes upon her cool exotic beauty, to finding some way, perhaps, of tricking her into staying over. And then ... who knew? Maybe he would be able to exploit that incredible sexual appetite of hers to make her do what he knew her prickly pride would never want her to do again: spend the night with him, in his bed, in his own home.

*   *   *

Ebony had some misgivings in the taxi on the way to the Carstairses' home. She wasn't sure what it was about the invitation from Mrs Carstairs that worried her, unless it was the way the woman had repeatedly assured her that Alan would not be there. Ebony understood why she kept making the assurance. No way would Ebony have accepted otherwise. Now, more than ever, she was taking pains to avoid him.

In just under two weeks she would be on her way to Paris.

Perhaps her misgivings were due to the fact that she didn't want to be anywhere that even *reminded* her of Alan. Out of sight was out of mind, they said. And that was partially true. She would never forget Alan, but not seeing him was easier than encounters like the other night. They only served to enslave her senses with memories of what she could experience when in his arms. And while she fully understood that physical pleasure without love left a bitter taste in the mouth, one didn't seem to remember that till afterwards.

She wanted no more afterwardses. Not ever.

The taxi stopped outside the high security fence that guarded the Carstairses' home. She paid the fare and alighted, drawing her black woollen cape around her black woollen trousers. Her mohair jumper was black too, but with pearls sewn in a flower pattern around the neck and across the padded shoulders. Her hair was braided, falling down the centre of her back in one long thick plait. She was only wearing a smattering of make-up.

Deirdre had said dinner would just be the two of them.

Using the keys still in her possession, she let herself in through the security gate and crunched up the gravel drive, glancing in fond memory at the fountain in the centre of the well-ordered gardens. She had used to like feeding the birds that flocked around that fountain in the spring. She used to like living in this house. It had seemed so warm compared to her growing-up years. Even the boarding-school Alan had sent her to was warm compared to those grim, lonely years. She'd actually felt loved for the first time in her life.

Loved...

Ebony ignored the contraction in her heart and stepped up on to the wide white-columned portico. The house itself was also white and looked relatively modest from street level, but actually had three levels which allowed it to hug the steeply sloped block as it dropped down to the shoreline of Double Bay. Besides the house itself, there was a terraced swimming-pool, a tennis court and a private jetty, Alan's small but luxury cruiser, *Man-About-Town*, moored not far off shore.

Ebony could have let herself in with her keys, but that would assume a casual intimacy with this house and its inhabitants which she'd lost four years before. She felt sorry that Alan's mother was slightly bewildered by her and Alan's public behaviour towards each other. Deirdre Carstairs had never been anything but kind to her since her son had brought her home as a shy, rather introverted girl of fifteen. Maybe Mrs Carstairs had been a little lonely at the time—Alan's sister had just left home. Whatever, the woman had welcomed Ebony with open arms and the two had become as close as Ebony's reserved nature had allowed.

Ebony was very fond of her. Which was why she could not refuse this invitation to dinner, despite having felt slightly uneasy about it from the start. Right at this moment, that uneasiness seemed to be increasing, which was ridiculous. Alan's car was not parked in front of the house where he always left it when he was home. He was away in Melbourne on business. Deirdre had told her as much only yesterday She was safe.

Shrugging off her edginess, she moved forward to press the front doorbell, sweeping her cape off in readiness for stepping into air-conditioning.

Bob answered the door. 'Hello, Miss Ebony,' he said, taking her cape as she stepped inside.

'Hello, Bob. What's on the menu for tonight? Another of your fabulous Italian dishes?'

'I don't know about fabulous, but Mr Alan won't eat anything else these days.'

Her panic was immediate. 'Mr Alan? But I thought——'

'Ebony, dear,' Deirdre Carstairs exclaimed as she rushed across the foyer, looking flustered but stylish in a pale blue shirtmaker dress that complemented her silver-grey hair. 'You're a bit early.'

'Mrs Carstairs, did I misunderstand? Bob implied just now that Alan would be here for dinner. You said that he was going to Melbourne tonight.'

Guilt was written all over the woman's face. 'Yes, I know I did, dear, but you see, Alan said that...well, he was sure that... Oh, dear, I was afraid this wouldn't work.'

'It already has, Mother,' Alan drawled as he joined them, looking casually elegant in an extremely modern suit of the palest blue-grey wool, made all the more modern looking by his teaming it with a white turtle-neck sweater. 'Ebony's here,' he stated smugly.

'Yes, but she's not happy about it. You've only got to look at her...'

Ebony would have liked to slice the smile from Alan's face with a meat cleaver. Instead, she assembled every ounce of composure she had, squashing any panic and controlling her rush of adrenalin with a couple of steadying breaths. Then she did the very opposite of what Alan would have been expecting. She smiled back at him.

'Did you think you had to lie to me to have the pleasure of my company? Silly man. You only ever had to ask nicely, Alan, didn't you know that? All that old antagonism was quite unnecessary. I'm very amenable when men are nice to me. Just ask Gary.'

It seemed hidden barbs were far more effective than meat cleavers, Ebony decided when she saw Alan's smile fade. But the icy fury that slipped into his eyes was unnerving, till she remembered he couldn't do a single damned thing in front of his mother. All she had to do to protect herself was keep Mrs Carstairs in full view for the entire evening.

The woman herself was at that moment looking a touch confused. Possibly she sensed the dark undercurrents between her son and his ward and wasn't quite sure how to take them. 'I... I only wanted to try to get you two to make up,' she said unhappily. 'Life's too short to be on bad terms when it's not necessary. Both of you have far too much pride!'

'Pride, Mother? Ebony has no pride.'

'Alan!'

'I only meant that I've never met a more modest model,' he amended with mock-apology. 'She has no conception of her extraordinary beauty, of the effect she has on the opposite sex. Why, only the other night, the chap sitting next to me at the fashion awards could hardly contain his drooling. It's amazing that she keeps such a cool head about her when so many men are willing to throw themselves at her feet.'

Her laughter was almost genuine. Alan throwing himself at her feet was a delightful image to contemplate. Too bad it would never be true.

'Ebony has always been a very sensible girl,' his mother praised. 'Now why are we standing around out here when we could be comfortable in the living-room? Dinner will be ready shortly, dear,' she went on as she linked arms with Ebony. 'And don't take any notice of Alan's stirring. He's out of practice being nice to you, I can see. Let's hope he finds his manners before the end of the evening.'

Now it was Alan who laughed, the sardonic sound drawing a frowning backwards glance from

Ebony. Immediately, their eyes locked, Alan's narrowed gaze promising all sorts of punishments for her, if and when he got the chance. 'Don't be concerned, Mother,' he called after them. 'By the end of the evening, butter won't melt in my mouth.'

CHAPTER FOUR

BY THE end of the evening, Alan wished he had died and gone to hell. Hell, he decided, was far preferable to sitting a few feet away from that witch, watching her eat, smelling that damned tantalising perfume she always wore, and not being able to touch her.

Perhaps if his subterfuge of being here when she hadn't expected it had *really* rattled her, he might have found some satisfaction, despite his own discomfort. But there she sat, unaware—or maybe *very* aware—of his torment, chatting away to his mother while throwing him the odd crumb of a casual comment every now and then, as well as the occasional glance.

Yes, he decided, hard blue eyes narrowing on that perfect profile. She *was* aware. Why else would she slide those seductive eyes his way with such sly regularity, if not to check that he was looking at her, wanting her, *needing* her?

Bitch, he thought as his loins began to ache. What I wouldn't give to wipe that cool composure from her face, to ravage those lush red lips as they deserve to be ravaged. He almost groaned aloud at the mental image that flashed into his mind. For he'd never experienced a woman as wild in bed as Ebony could be. Or as abandoned.

Which was her fascination, of course, he finally accepted. Why else was he compelled to keep coming back to her for more when there was no love lost between them, when she made no concessions to his male ego, when she didn't bother to hide her contempt for him?

Contempt?

He frowned darkly into his coffee, having never thought of Ebony's feelings for him in quite such derisive terms before. Oh, he knew she hated him. But he'd always imagined that was a reverse reaction to the schoolgirl crush she'd once harboured, a pride thing. No one liked being rejected as he'd once rejected her. Yet underlying that hate had remained the chemistry that had flared between them that night in the library, a chemistry that had survived their mutual antagonism.

It was a very explosive chemistry, Alan conceded ruefully. Explosive and volatile, sometimes bordering on violent. One day, he suspected it would totally self-destruct. In fact, it was probably heading for that moment right now...

'What do you think, Alan?'

Alan blinked once before focusing on the object of his mental rummaging. She was looking at him with wide, almost innocent eyes, her head tipped sideways as she had used to do as a young girl.

The blackest feeling of guilt swamped him. She's still little more than a girl, he agonised. God, what have I done to her? What do I keep doing to her?

But then he glimpsed the beginning of a very adult, almost devilish glitter in those eyes, and every vestige of guilt vanished. He would have her in his bed tonight if it was the last thing he did!

'About what?' he returned silkily, secure in the knowledge that she would not have seen anything of his inner torture on his face. His earlier slip-up when she'd taunted him about Stevenson had put him on his guard. She had not coaxed any visible reaction from him over dinner, and she would not do so now. 'Sorry, but I wasn't listening.'

'It's not like you to daydream,' she said with a small, teasing smile.

His shrug was offhand. 'My concentration suffers when I'm tired.'

'Alan's been working too hard lately,' Deirdre put in. 'Sometimes he works all night.'

'Really?' Ebony arched her eyebrows. 'Well, he always was a one for all-nighters, Mrs Carstairs. Remember when I first came to live here with you? A couple of nights a week at least he didn't make it home.'

Alan tensed, knowing exactly what Ebony was referring to—not work, but his three-year affair with Adrianna. He had used to stay over at her apartment quite regularly, a fact which clearly had not escaped Ebony, despite her being in school most of the time. But all that had ended when Adrianna had fallen in love with another man and married him.

'He'll never change, Mrs Carstairs,' Ebony went on, a touch sharply. 'Old habits die hard.' Now she lanced him with a vicious look that only he could see. 'Unless someone takes a firm hand and makes them die. Perhaps it's time you found a woman to marry, Alan. You're not getting any younger.'

His smile was velvet around steel. 'I assure you, my dear Ebony, if and when I find a woman I *want* to marry, I will.'

'Huh!' his mother scoffed at him. 'You haven't even looked at another woman since Adrianna married that McLean fellow. If you think she'll ever get a divorce, then think again! The woman's besotted with the man.'

'I realise that,' Alan said tautly. 'Believe me when I say I am not waiting in the wings, hoping Adrianna will one day divorce her husband. Especially not with a baby and another on the way. What on earth do you think I am? A home-wrecker?'

'No, of course I don't,' his mother said impatiently. 'But I wish you'd give consideration to being a home-*maker*! Ebony's right. You're thirty-four years old. Time you were married and having babies of your own. I'd like to have grandchildren before I get too old to enjoy them.'

'I'm sure Vicki will give you some. Eventually.'

'Vicki! She hasn't a maternal bone in her body. As for that layabout she's living with... I doubt he's got it in him to father a child! But we're getting off the point here. The subject under discussion is *your* fathering a child. Or don't you want children?'

Did he or didn't he? He'd never thought he did. He'd always been too busy, too wrapped up in saving the family business, then in expanding it, making it into a success. One of the reasons he'd proposed marriage to Adrianna was because, at the time, she hadn't wanted children.

It was ironic that the moment she'd really fallen in love she hadn't been able to wait to have a baby. Her son, Christopher, had been born nine months to the day after she'd married Bryce McLean.

Now there was a lucky bastard, winning the heart of a woman like Adrianna. If only she'd fallen in love with *him* instead.

His mind turned inwards to the way Ebony treated him. No man would ever win that witch's heart, he thought savagely.

Alan looked up to find both women were watching him, expectant expressions on their faces.

'Will I be hung, drawn and quartered if I say I have no great yearning for children?'

Deirdre Carstairs sighed. 'I should have known. Well, it's up to you, Ebony. Your children will feel like grandchildren to me. I hope you haven't any objection to eventually having babies.'

'I'd love to have a dozen babies,' she said with such apparent sincerity that Alan was stunned. 'I hated being an only child. When I have a family, it will be a very large one.'

'And spoil that perfect figure of yours?' he asked, unable to eliminate the derision in his voice.

She turned cold black eyes upon him. 'Having a baby is worth a little figure-spoiling.'

'Not according to most of the models I've come across. One hint of pregnancy and they're off for a termination before you can say Jack Robinson.'

'I do not believe in abortion,' she stated categorically.

'Not till it's you who's pregnant, you mean,' he jeered.

Again, her eyes speared icy daggers his way. 'I would never have an abortion. Not in normal circumstances. Other women can do as they please, but I wouldn't feel right about it. That is my belief and nothing and no one would ever sway me.'

Alan stared deep into her eyes and knew that what she said was true. He felt a grudging admiration for her. If there was one thing admirable about Ebony it was the implacable nature of her spirit. She had emotional strength. He would give her that. Too bad she often used that strength in battle against him. He would much rather she had a softer, more pliable nature.

Or would he?

A slow, sardonic smile creased his mouth. No... Much as her stubborn pride and outright defiance infuriated him at times, he would not trade her fighting ways for anything. There was nothing more pleasurable than his triumph after finally subduing her sexually, or the intense satisfaction he gained when his physically stronger body eventually gained the upper hand.

'You find something amusing in what I said?' she challenged icily.

'Oh, dear,' Deirdre broke in, her voice worried. 'Please don't you two get into an argument. You were both going along splendidly there for a while.

Look, let's forget all about babies and talk about something else.'

'By all means,' Alan agreed curtly. 'I never brought them up in the first place.'

The loud banging of a door and noisily approaching footsteps brought all their attention to the archway that led from the dining-room back into the main living area.

Ebony, for one, was glad of the distraction. She'd been about to murder Alan, the insensitive swine. But she supposed he could never have guessed that the most treasured dream she'd ever had was to marry him and have his babies.

'Vicki!' Deirdre exclaimed when the unexpected visitor marched into the room. 'Whatever are you doing here at this hour?'

Vicki was an attractive but not beautiful woman. She was tall, with brown hair and blue eyes, like her brother; confident and assertive, like her brother; unconsciously selfish, like her brother.

'I've had it with Alistair!' she announced and, dragging out an empty chair, plopped herself down at the dining-table. 'He's the most stupid man it's ever been my misfortune to live with.'

'Then why keep living with him?' Alan remarked drily.

Vicki pouted, then laughed. 'Because he's good in bed?'

'Vicki!' her mother protested. 'We have company!'

'Ebony's not company,' Vicki retorted. 'She's family, aren't you, sweetie?'

Ebony could not help but notice that Alan looked momentarily uncomfortable at this remark. So he *did* feel some measure of guilt over her. Good!

She gave his sister a sickly smile. 'How nice of you to say so.'

'Nonsense. It's not nice at all. It's true. You've been a better daughter to Mum here than I've ever been. Too bad you had to get on your high horse and leave like you did. Not necessary, you know. My old money-bags of a brother didn't miss a few thousand dollars. He probably gives more to charity every year than he ever spent on you, honeybun. Still, I suppose a gal has to have her pride, which is why I walked out on Alistair tonight.'

'You mean you've come home to live?' her mother gasped.

Vicki suddenly looked crestfallen. Her chin began to quiver. They all stared at her. Alan's sister never ever cried.

'I ... I guess so.' Gathering herself, she lifted her chin defiantly. 'Alistair needs to be taught a lesson!'

'In what?' her brother asked a touch warily.

'In understanding what a woman wants.'

'Which is?' Alan probed.

'Love. Romance. *Consideration*!' And she promptly burst into tears.

Her mother was up and mothering in one second flat, quite in her element as she made excuses and carted Vicki off to her old bedroom.

When Ebony had gone to stand up to see if she could help, Deirdre Carstairs had waved her back down again. 'You stay and keep Alan company,' she'd whispered across Vicki's bowed, weeping head.

'Poor thing,' Ebony murmured once the other two women were out of earshot.

'She made her bed,' Alan said. 'Now she'll have to lie in it.'

His ruthless lack of pity and understanding fired Ebony's temper. 'What a rotten thing to say about your own sister! Don't you care that she's hurting?'

'Vicki will be thirty next birthday,' Alan returned mercilessly. 'She's had more Alistairs in her life than I have fingers and toes, all of whom she's been madly in love with, and all of whom have used her shamelessly. One would have hoped that she'd have grown up a little by now, and that her judgement of men would have improved.'

'It's hard to be analytical and logical when one's emotions are involved. Or don't you know anything about emotions, Alan?'

His smile was vaguely smug as he surveyed her high colour. Ebony recognised that this was what he'd been trying to do all night—provoke her into having an open altercation with him. Why, she wasn't sure. Bloody-mindedness, she supposed. And he'd succeeded.

Yet somehow she didn't care. She was going to have her say; she was going to tell him what she thought of him. It would probably be her last chance and it would do her soul good to get it all off her chest.

'No, you wouldn't. Not you!' She threw down her serviette and stood up. 'Why, you're no better than Vicki's Alistair. When have you ever given a woman love, or romance, or consideration? Do you even know what any of those things mean? I wonder now if you were ever in love with Adrianna Winslow, if you're capable of loving any woman. I've certainly never seen any evidence of it. Because loving someone means giving a little. All you can do is take, Alan!'

His laughter stunned her, as did his applause. 'Wonderful! You should be an actress, not a model. If I didn't know you better, I would almost think you meant some of that.'

She simply stared at him, feeling sick to her stomach. Had she ever loved this cruel, heartless man?

Slowly, he too rose to his feet, taking his time as he moved round behind his chair and scooped it in to the table. He stood behind it, his long, elegant fingers curled over the curved wooden back, his hard blue eyes narrowing with the most appallingly explicit desire as they roved over her body. Immediately, she felt that curl of answering desire within her, and was disgusted by it.

'If you touch me,' she said shakily, 'I'll scream this house down.'

'Will you?'

'Try me.'

She meant it; Alan could see that. It surprised then angered him. Who did she think she was, deciding when he could and could not touch her? She was his whenever he wanted her, damn it. Hadn't he proved that to her time and time again? God, but he was tired of her games, tired of the way she kept his desire dangling, just because it amused her perverse nature. Or was she still punishing him for having rejected her once?

Yes, that was probably it. No doubt he'd made a big mistake about her that night in the library. She hadn't been an innocent back then at all. She'd already been a little tramp, kissing him like that, using her Lolita talents to tempt him so severely that afterwards he hadn't been able to get her out of his mind. Even now, after having had her countless times, he hadn't tired of her. One would have thought he would have been able to rid himself of this obsessive need by now. But it was stronger than ever.

'Perhaps I will,' he said in a low, threatening voice, and began walking towards her.

'Everyone finished in here?' Bob asked, his sudden appearance bringing a frustrated scowl to Alan's face and a shudder of relief from Ebony.

He'd been going to kiss her, she realised shakily. And she wouldn't have been able to do a thing about it. Bob's arrival had come just in the nick of time.

'Yes, Bob,' she said. 'It was all lovely.'

'It certainly was,' Alan agreed, having gathered himself quickly. 'Come, Ebony, we'll go and see what's become of Vicki and Mother. Then I'll see you home.'

When Ebony hesitated, Alan came forward, all smiles, taking her elbow and steering her none too gently from the dining-room and across the living area.

'Let me go,' she hissed, her efforts to dislodge her arm from his grip unsuccessful.

'Stop acting like a cantankerous child,' he hissed back. 'Do you want Bob to see you for what you really are?'

'Which is?'

'Well, certainly not the sweet little thing you've convinced my whole family you are!'

'Is that so? Well, maybe Bob and your family could do with a bit of enlightenment of *your* character as well? You're hardly holier-than-thou. Maybe I should tell them what's been keeping you away all those nights this past year.'

'You won't do that,' he ground out as he urged her down the steps that led to the next level, and the bedrooms. But he didn't turn down the corridor to where his mother's and Vicki's bedrooms were, sweeping her instead round the other way and into his own bedroom. Her cry of protest was muffled when his hand closed over her mouth and he kicked the door shut behind him.

She bit him. Hard.

'You bitch!' he gasped, flicking his hand madly before trying to suck the pain away. His blue eyes blazed as he glared hate at her.

'You're lucky I didn't do you more damage. Keep away from me, Alan,' she warned. 'I don't want you any more.'

Now he laughed.

'I mean it!'

'Might I remind you you've said all this before.'

'This time it's different.'

'How is it different?'

Ebony was about to throw Gary and Paris in his face again when she stopped. That would be a stupid thing to do. Alan in a jealous rage was both frightening and insidiously attractive to her. Desperately she searched around for something to say. Anything!

'You're beginning to bore me,' she bit out, not realising till the words were out that it was an even more stupid thing to say.

Alan's face darkened, then filled with scorn. 'Is that so? Well, you could have fooled me. Only the other night you couldn't get enough of me.'

She flushed fiercely, shame a bitter sword in her heart. 'That was then,' she went on, digging her own grave even further. 'This is now.'

'So it is,' he smiled. 'Shall we see how different now is, then? Shall I give you a little test?'

Ebony backed up against the door when he took a step towards her, her hand reaching blindly for the knob. She found it at the same time as his hands closed tightly around both her wrists, holding her in a grip of iron while he pressed his body up against hers, his head dipping to kiss not her mouth but her neck.

A shudder ran through her.

His mouth travelled slowly up the long white column of her throat, his sipping kisses soft and moist and seductive. They moved along her jawline, up over her ears, across her temples to press gently against her suddenly closed eyelids. By the time he worked his way down to the corner of her mouth, she was aching to part her lips to invite the sort of kiss that could only end one way.

'No,' she moaned, in protest against her own flaring passion.

'Stop being silly,' he rasped against her quivering lips. 'You still want me as much as I want you. There's no use denying it, Ebony. I can feel you trembling already.'

Sensing her inability to struggle at that moment, he let go of her wrists, his hands moving up under her jumper while his mouth continued to hover over hers.

'This is what you want, isn't it?' he tempted, stroking her braless breasts till she was really trembling.

But not entirely from desire. Despair was sending her crashing down a tortuous path she'd never been before. For the first time she could not totally block out the ugliness of it all, the sordidness behind the sensuality. A feeling of intense desolation flooded in, tears filling her eyes. She made a choking sound.

Alan's abrupt withdrawal bewildered her for a second. Her soggy lashes fluttered upwards, her blurred vision gradually taking in an Alan she had never seen before. He looked quite shattered.

'You're . . . you're crying,' he said, obviously shaken.

She blinked, gulped, and said nothing. She couldn't. The tears were still running down her face and the back of her throat. Yet now that he'd stopped touching her, she felt oddly desolate, which was a perverse reaction, given her devastation of a moment ago, not to mention her ongoing weeping.

'I . . . I don't *like* you crying,' he went on in a type of angry confusion. 'Stop it!'

Now she began to laugh as well as sob, bringing her rapidly to the edge of hysteria. His stinging slap across her face sent her mouth gasping and her eyes flinging wide.

'Stop it,' he groaned into the sudden electric silence, his face a tortured mask.

Her answer was a single strangled sob.

'God, Ebony,' he shuddered. 'I'm sorry. Sorry...'

And then he was cupping her stunned face, pressing impassioned lips to her eyelids, licking the tears away, tracing the red imprint of his hand on her cheek with trembling fingertips, whispering more wildly apologetic words that sent her heart soaring and her defences crashing. Her own hands lifted to his face, inviting him to take her mouth in a proper kiss.

His hesitation was only brief, and then he was crushing her to him, kissing her till their breathing had gone haywire. The love she had hopelessly tried to destroy came rushing back, firing her with the need to express that love in the only way he had ever let her.

'Make love to me, Alan,' she cried huskily. 'Make love to me, Alan,' she cried huskily. 'Make love to me . . .'

With a raw groan of desire, he swept her up into his arms and carried her swiftly to his bed. Within no time they were both naked, both in the throes of a passion that knew nothing but each other. It was no wonder that they didn't hear Deirdre's first soft tap on the heavy door.

CHAPTER FIVE

DEIRDRE was worried. When she'd returned to the kitchen to make Vicki a drink of hot chocolate she'd noticed the dining- and living-rooms were empty. Bob had told her that he thought Ebony had gone home and Mr Alan to bed. But Ebony's black cape was still hanging on the coat stand in the foyer.

It wasn't till after Deirdre had taken the drink back to Vicki that the idea presented itself that Ebony and Alan might have had another row, with an upset Ebony forgetting to take her cape when she left. The more she thought about that possibility, the more she was convinced it was right. The atmosphere between them tonight had been as fraught with tension as ever before, and it was all Alan's fault. He'd tried to needle Ebony from the moment she'd arrived.

Annoyed with him, Deirdre went along to his room to confront him with what had happened. Already she'd knocked once, with no answer, yet she could swear she could hear noises coming from inside.

Exasperation joined her irritation. If Alan thought she would just go away if he ignored her knocking, then he had another think coming. She meant to give him a piece of her mind if he'd been fighting with Ebony again.

Her second knock was quite loud, as was her voice asking if he was in there. But she waited no more than a couple of seconds before barging right in, intent on not letting her son brush her off so rudely.

Shock galvanised her to the spot in the open doorway, her fingers freezing on the knob. For there was no doubting what she had just interrupted her son doing. His state of undress, combined with his hurried rolling sideways and scooping a sheet upwards, was telling enough. But it was the sight of his open-mouthed bed-partner that caused Deirdre Carstairs's heart to stop beating.

'Ebony!' she gasped aloud, unable to believe what she was seeing.

The girl herself gave a choked cry and turned to bury her face in the pillow. Alan closed his eyes momentarily before throwing his mother a black look.

'Maybe that will teach you not to come into a man's bedroom unannounced,' he growled.

'But... but I *did* knock,' she wailed, appalled both with the situation and all the thoughts it sent tumbling through her mind. My God, how long had this been going on?

A long time, she realised with a mother's sudden intuition. Maybe even longer...

Nausea rose in her throat, and she swallowed convulsively. Dear God, not that long, she prayed.

Immediately, she turned on the person who, on age alone, had to be mostly to blame. 'Oh, Alan, how *could* you?'

His reaction staggered her.

'How could *I*? My God, that's rich, that is. How could *I*?' he repeated, then laughed. 'Oh, get out, Mother, before I say things you won't want to hear. Get out and take all your presumptions with you because I'm not going to deny a thing. Yes, I heartlessly seduced your poor darling sweet little Ebony. Yes, I betrayed the sacred trust her father gave her. Yes, I'm a wicked depraved lecher. Will it make you happy to believe that?'

Ebony wanted to bury her face in the pillow forever when she heard Alan's indirect but scathing condemnation of her character, her despair so great it was beyond despair. It was death. He had finally sentenced her love to death. A little while before, when he'd apologised and started making love to her, she had thought he loved her. But no...she'd been wrong...again.

Her pride-filled spirit had not died, however. It was, if anything, made stronger by this ultimate of betrayals. Steeling herself, she rolled over and levered herself upright, tossing her long hair back as she swung her legs over the side of the bed and bent down to begin drawing on her scattered clothes.

Not a word was uttered by anyone as she pulled on her panties. Not a single word. She sensed that both Alan and his mother were watching her go about her coolly composed dressing in a state of stunned silence, but she refused to show any distress.

At last, with head held high, she started to walk from the room, stopping only briefly to bestow a sad little smile on the pale-faced woman standing with her back against the open door, her hand still on the doorknob. 'I'm sorry, Mrs Carstairs. Really, I am. Please don't see me out. Goodnight. Thank you for the lovely dinner.' And without giving Alan so much as a parting glance, she swept from the room.

Alan's mouth had dropped open with her blasé boldness, her total lack of shame. *He* was the one who was left with the shame, and the guilt, *and* the frustration. God, if only he'd thought to lock the damned door. Then he wouldn't be lying here with his mother looking at him as if he were the original Bluebeard, or worse!

'Should...shouldn't you go after her?' she managed to say.

'Not bloody likely. And before you start in on me,' he went on testily, 'Ebony was not dragged into this bed by the hair on her head. She came willingly enough. And it's not the first time, either.'

'So I gathered by your earlier comments.' His mother glanced daggers at him again. 'Yet you are the older party here, Alan, and I am not impressed by your trying to paint Ebony as some sort of scarlet woman. She is nothing of the kind! It would seem that you have—much to your discredit—taken advantage of the girl's one-time hero-worship of you.'

She dismissed his startled look with a scornful wave of her hand. 'Oh, yes, I knew about that. Do you think I go around here with my eyes shut? As for your both trying to hide this affair from me by pretending not to like one another... I find such deception most reprehensible. But once again, I heap most of the blame on you, Alan. I'm sure it was not Ebony's idea. I can only conclude also that this intimacy began when society would have frowned on such a relationship.'

'It did not!' he defended fiercely. 'I didn't touch her till she turned twenty-one!'

His mother looked surprised, then relieved, then confused. 'Then why all the secrecy? Why not be open about your relationship? Good lord, Alan, I would like nothing better than for you and Ebony to marry.'

'Which is exactly why I didn't want you to find out about us,' he snapped. 'Ebony would never marry me for starters. And I damned well would never marry her!'

'Why not?'

'God...'

'Tell me, Alan. I think I have a right to know. The girl was placed in *my* care as well as yours. I worry about her. She's a very vulnerable type of girl.'

Vulnerable? Was his mother kidding? Hadn't she seen her swan out of here just now, unmoved at having been discovered *in flagrante delicto* with the man who was not only her legal guardian, but twelve years older than herself? Hell, Ebony was as hard as her name!

'You want the truth,' he challenged. 'The whole unvarnished truth?'

Deirdre squared her shoulders and her chin. 'I do.'

'So be it, then. So be it...'

Ebony did not cry till she reached the safety of her flat. Then it all poured out, all the hurt and the pain and the shame. She would never forget the look of horror on Alan's mother's face when she had walked into that bedroom. Never! Ebony had never felt so low in all her life. How she had got herself out of there with some shreds of dignity intact she had no idea. But she had, thank God.

As for Alan... She had never hated him as much as she had when he'd failed to defend her, when he'd destroyed his mother's good opinion of her. She'd never pretended to be a saint. But she wasn't a slut either. She was merely a woman, made weak by a love that had been doomed from the start. Now, there was no one left who thought well of her, who cared for her.

No one except Gary...

Ebony stood up and went to get her luggage. Time to start packing, she thought. Time to escape this torment for good.

The doorbell ringing sent her into a momentary panic till she remembered she was in control here. No one could get in unless she let them in.

Initially, she ignored it, till the insistent buzzing nearly drove her mad. Only Alan would be so persistent. Any normal person would have given up and gone away. In the end, she marched over and flicked the switch on the intercom. 'Yes, Alan?'

'I need to talk to you,' he ground out.

'Well, I don't want to talk to you.'

'So I gathered. Look, I regret what happened earlier. I should have locked that damned door. But I straightened Mother out about a few things, and she doesn't think badly of you. Quite the contrary. I'm the one she tore strips off. She's cast you in the role of the wronged woman. She actually thinks you're in love with me.'

Ebony sucked in a startled breath, then laughed. 'I hope you straightened her out about that as well,' she scorned.

'I tried. She wouldn't listen. In the end I decided to let her think whatever she liked if it made her feel better.'

'How gallant of you! And did you also let her believe *you're* in love with *me*?'

'Her mind did start going along those paths. Eventually,' he added drily.

'And you didn't want to disillusion her about her beloved son's morals, is that it?'

'Something like that.'

'You bastard,' she bit out. 'You stinking rotten bastard. Why didn't you tell her the truth? That the only thing you've ever wanted from me is sex. It's why you're here now. You think you can take up where you left off. But you're wrong, Alan. I'm finished with you,' she stated harshly. 'For good!'

'Stop being so melodramatic. It doesn't suit you. But I can understand you might be a little upset. And I'm sorry.'

'He's sorry! My God, can you repeat that? I'd like to tape it for posterity. An apology from Alan Carstairs to his slut of a mistress.'

'Don't call yourself that!'

'Why? It's how you think of me, isn't it?'

'God, Ebony, can't we discuss this in private? Let me come up. It's cold out here.'

'It'll be even colder in here, believe me. Just go home, Alan. And don't come back. I don't ever want to set eyes on you again.'

'You don't mean that.'

'Don't I? We'll see, Alan, we'll see.'

'Yes, we certainly will!' he snarled, and stormed off.

Alan sat in his car for quite some time afterwards, fuming. In love with him, was she? His mother was mad! That witch didn't know *how* to love. She was a vampire, a blood-sucking vampire, not content unless she drove a man to distraction.

And yet...

His gut twisted as he recalled her tears earlier on that night. God, but they'd affected him. Not with triumph as he'd once imagined, but with shock and real dismay. Ebony crying did not fit the image he had of her. Yet her tears represented some real evidence behind his mother's belief that Ebony was in love with him. Why should she cry unless her emotions were deeply involved?

And just now...

Was her bitter sarcasm another symptom of frustrated love? Had he finally driven her to the point where she couldn't bear to see him again because it hurt her too much?

His whole stomach turned over with the possibility. Goddamn it, maybe his mother *was* right!

Alan gripped the steering-wheel, his head spinning. He remembered that his first reaction to such an outrageous idea had been a mocking denial.

'You're crazy!' he had told his mother.

But once he'd revealed that incident four years before in the library, his mother had been adamant that she was right, steadfastly resisting any suggestion that Ebony was nothing better than a tramp and a tease, even shrugging off his telling her about Ebony's reputation with other men.

'You shouldn't believe everything you hear, Alan,' she'd rebuked. 'As for when Ebony kissed you in the library...you have no evidence she wasn't a virgin back then. I'm sure she was, just as I'm sure she was already in love with you. Can't you see that?'

He hadn't. 'A girl of eighteen? In love with a man of thirty? Oh, come, now, Mother. Next thing you'll be telling me I was in love with her.'

'No. I know better than that. You were in love with Adrianna.'

'Well, no, actually... I wasn't.'

'You *weren't*?'

'I was having an affair with her, but I wasn't in love with her, any more than she was in love with me. We were close friends as well as business associates, and we were both lonely. That's the total sum of our relationship.'

'But you asked her to marry you.'

'Yes...'

'Why?'

Alan had no option but to tell the truth. 'To protect Ebony.'

'To...protect...Ebony...'

'Don't look at me like that, Mother. It was as much your fault as mine.'

'How, for heaven's sake?'

'Remember that white lace dress you put her in for her eighteenth birthday party?'

'Yes, why? She looked lovely in it.'

'And incredibly sexy. I took one look at her that night and wanted her. It's as simple as that. Suddenly, she was no longer that schoolgirl who'd been flitting in and out of my life for nearly three years. She was, body-wise, a woman—a beautiful and highly desirable woman. And I wanted her.' He shuddered with the memory. 'God, I've never felt such desire, or such guilt, in my entire life.'

'Oh, Alan...'

'I thought if I had a wife in my bed every night, then I would be able to cure my lust. I think Adrianna was going to say yes, too. But as you know, she met Bryce McLean in the outback after her plane crashed, and there went my plans to be noble. Shortly after she got married, Ebony kissed me and all hell broke loose.'

'I see...'

'I hope so. Look, I did what I thought was right by forcing her to leave like that, but I never did get over wanting her. It got worse too as she grew in both her beauty and her sexuality. It killed me to hear about her multitude of affairs. So when she virtually offered herself to me the night of her twenty-first birthday party, I took her. And I've kept on taking her every damned time I've felt like it. And you know what? She's never said no, never wanted anything from me but what I wanted from her. Pure unadulterated sex. So don't go telling me she loves me, because I don't buy it. The girl's sex mad. I'll warrant I'm not the only man to grace her bed, though I'll kill the bastard or bastards if I ever get my hands on them.'

His mother had looked at him then with shock and pity on her face. 'Oh, Alan, you just can't see, can you?'

'Can't see what?'

'You're in love with her too!'

He'd laughed at her at the time.

But now he wasn't so sure. Could this be love, this gnawing at his insides, this ghastly regret that he hadn't made Ebony stay earlier on, hadn't held her close and told his mother that yes, she was his woman and he was proud of that fact?

Adrianna had once told him what he felt for Ebony was love, that he was blinded to his real feelings by the intensity of his passion. Desire, she'd said, had a way of tricking people, making fools of them.

Well, it certainly kept making a fool of him. Did that mean he was really in love with the woman? There! He had at last admitted it. Ebony was a woman, not a girl. At least he didn't have to feel guilty about that part any longer.

But what kind of woman?

Ah, yes . . . there lay the crux of the matter. What kind of woman was she?

Images tantalised his brain, and his body. Was it love that made her make love like that? Or sheer decadence? Did he really care?

Yes, came the astonishing answer. *God, yes, he did*!

A grimly determined expression thinned his mouth as he lent forward and fired the engine. He'd give her a couple of days to calm down, and then . . . then he'd set about finding out the answers to the many questions tonight had raised.

For he could not go on like this, he realised, his nerves stretched tight, his mind and body rarely at peace. If he didn't find some answer soon, something would have to give. He was a man, not a machine. And there was just so much a man could take.

CHAPTER SIX

EBONY rang Gary first thing the next morning, before he left the hotel.

'You haven't changed your mind again, have you?' he groaned, once he knew who was on the other end of the line.

'Far from it. I wanted to confirm our arrangements. We fly out Tuesday week, is that it?'

'Yes. I was only able to get you a holiday visa to start with, but once the fashion houses in Paris get a gander at you you'll have work offers coming out of your ears.'

'I'm not worried about working. I just have to get away from here.'

'You still having trouble with Carstairs?'

'Mmm.'

'One day, you'll have to tell me the whole gruesome story.'

'Maybe.'

Gary sighed. 'I'm your friend, love. I won't breathe a word of anything you tell me to anyone else. Are you worried the gossip rags might get a hold of it?'

'Hardly. They don't need real facts for a story. They make it up as they go along. I'm already supposed to have slept with every photographer I've ever met.'

'You should see some of the stuff they've printed about me!'

'All of which is probably true.'

'Of course,' Gary laughed. 'Doesn't hurt my career either. Amazing how many women want to be photographed by bad boy Stevenson. I wouldn't think a bit of reported spice has hurt your career, either.'

'Maybe my career hasn't suffered from the gossip, Gary, but my private life has.'

'You mean Carstairs *believes* all that rubbish they write about you?'

'Not only believes it but thrives on it, I think. He likes me bad.'

'Sounds like a bit of a rotten egg himself, Ebony. You're well rid of him. You *are* rid of him, aren't you?'

'I am now.'

'Good. Now what about your agency? What have you told them?'

'Just that I'm going on an extended working holiday overseas and won't be available for work for three months, starting next Monday. That way, I can leave my options open. Not that they were happy about it. They've had to cancel a couple of engagements I had, as well as turn down several new offers. Still, they'll survive. They have plenty of other good models on their books screaming out for work.'

'What about your flat?'

'I was going to put it in the hands of an agent to rent out, but I don't think I will now. I can't face the hassle. Besides, if I did that I'd have to store all my things, which would be time-consuming and expensive. I'm just going to shut it up and have the neighbours keep an eye on the place. If I decide to stay in Paris, I might have to fly back and sell up everything.'

'Yes, you could do that. As you say, no need to rush things. The main thing is to just get away for a while.'

'I can't wait,' she said with feeling.

'Good. Well, I'll ring you later in the week. We'll go to dinner somewhere.'

'I'd like that. Now I must away to the gym. I've a shoot on Monday for a fashion magazine. A swimwear layout, would you believe? In the dead of winter, of course. When else? Not that I mind, really. It's good to be busy. I've got a job every day this week.'

'I've a few appointments myself. Maybe we should leave the dinner till Friday night.'

'Yes, I think that might be wise.'

'How about dinner here in my room? We could have an intimate little candlelit meal and you could tell me all, without danger of being overheard.'

Ebony's laughter was softly rueful. 'You haven't given up on me yet, have you, Gary?'

'Oh, I think I have a realistic view when it comes to my favourite ex.'

'I hope so. One step out of line next Friday night and you might be having Security in your room, not Room Service.'

'You have my word of honour that I will honour your honour.'

'Gary,' she chuckled drily, 'you have no honour.'

'I realise that, love, but you have enough for both of us.'

'Do I?' Suddenly, her voice began to crack.

'You know you do. I can't think of another girl who looks like you, who was living alone and moving in circles you moved in, and who would still be a virgin at twenty. It took every bit of my worldly wiles to get you into bed that first time. And even then I remember you cried for a whole day afterwards. I'll bet my bottom dollar that other than that fool, Carstairs, there hasn't been another man in your life since then. Am I right?'

'Yes,' she choked out.

'Hell, but I feel like going over there and telling that bastard off. How dare he think wicked things about you? You're an angel. The man's a raving lunatic, or blind, or stupid, or all three!'

'No, Gary, I'm not an angel,' she denied unhappily. 'I'm not an angel at all. In fact, I sometimes wonder if I haven't created most of my problems myself...'

'What nonsense! Now don't you start blaming yourself, sweetie. You're a good girl and, if the man's not smart enough to see that, then there's no hope for him. Forget the fool! Believe me, once you're out of his life *he'll* forget *you*. I know his type. He'll have some other sexy little thing he thinks badly of in bed with him before you can say lickety-split. He doesn't want love, Ebony. He only wants sex. Take my word for it. Now, off to your gym and don't give the crumb another thought!'

Not giving Alan another thought was impossible. But Ebony kept herself busy enough over the weekend to stop herself from cracking up. She exercised, cleaned, gave her hair a special treatment, packed, forced some food down herself, listened to Jimmy Barnes, watched *Pretty Woman* for the third time, and tried not to cry too much. Puffy eyes did not look good on a model.

But always at the back of her mind was the fear that Alan would show up at any time, pressing her buzzer and pressuring her to see him again. And while she was determined not to—and quite confident that she would not give in—she knew such an encounter would upset her all over again.

Saturday and Sunday came and went, however, without any sign of him. Perversely, Ebony found this upsetting in itself. He'd implied he would not let her go, but it seemed he'd had second thoughts about that. Gary's assertion that Alan would quickly forget her seemed to be coming true. It underlined the shallow nature of his feelings for her, the lack of any real depth or caring. That should have been some comfort, some justification that what she was doing was right. Yet Ebony found little to feel happy about when she finally went to bed on Sunday night. All she felt was wretched and lonely.

Monday dawned blessedly dry, but there was not a skerrick of warmth in the sun. The photographs were to be taken on Bondi Beach and the company who'd contracted her had thankfully organised a caravan for her to dress and shelter in between takes. Since she had a dozen different suits to model, this was more a necessity than a luxury.

Actually, she hadn't done a swimwear shoot in ages, mainly because of her condition of only modelling black clothing these days. Most swimwear was colourful. But this particular sportswear company had created a new line to cash in on the idea that swimwear could double as sophisticated body-suits for evening wear. They were starting with an all black range, which featured daring necklines, a lot of stretch lace and net, and quite a bit of beading. Built into each crotch was a clever, velcro-type seam to facilitate the wearer's going to the bathroom without completely undressing.

Ebony could not imagine any right-thinking person actually wearing the costumes in the water, and fortunately the photographer seemed to agree. He kept her out of the surf, draping her across rocks, having her lie in the sand, even bringing a sleek silver Porsche down on to the beach so he could take shots of her beside it, in it, and on top of it.

It was while she was lying on the roof of the car, her face lifted to the watery sun, eyes shut, her long dark hair spread out in a circle on the thankfully warm silver metal, that Ebony felt the first prickling awareness of being watched.

She tried telling herself that of course she was being watched. Even in the middle of winter, Bondi

Beach was never deserted. Surfboard riders in wet-suits still came to catch waves; joggers and power walkers strutted their stuff along the esplanade; overseas tourists came to see first-hand what they had only ever seen in a brochure or on a postcard. Bondi was, after all, Sydney's most famous beach.

But it wasn't the curious gazes of accidental passers-by and tourists that were making the hairs on the back of Ebony's neck stand on end. She was sure of that. Someone was watching her with an intensity that was being telegraphed to her through the air waves, someone with whom she had a close emotional and physical bond.

'Alan,' she breathed, and sat bolt upright, wide black eyes darting around.

'Oh, for Pete's sake!' the photographer exclaimed frustratedly from where he was standing on the hood of the car. 'I just had the greatest shot in my sights and you damned well moved. What gives, Ebony? It's not like you to be skittish.'

'I . . . I had this feeling,' she said shakily. 'I thought someone was watching . . .'

The photographer gave a dry, disbelieving laugh. 'Honey, in that rig-out, the eyes of every red-blooded male within five hundred yards are watching you. Now lie back down, like a good girl, and let's get this wrapped up. The light's beginning to go.'

It was too, despite being only three in the afternoon. But the sun set early on an eastern beach when the city behind it blocked out the sun's rays.

Ebony lay back down, extra-conscious now that the stretch-lace costume was semi-transparent where her curves stretched the material, her areolae and nipples partially visible through the thinnish lace. A blush of embarrassment coloured her cheeks, which surprised her. Over the years she'd become rather nonchalant about showing off her body. Familiarity did breed a certain contempt and she had ceased to be worried by the odd semi-nude shot, as long as it was tasteful.

Suddenly, however, she didn't like to think strange men were ogling her body. Even the photographer was making her uncomfortable, yet she had worked with him many times before and he was one of the best. A real professional. But he was also one of the men her name had been linked with at one time, simply because he had been able to coax a sensuality from her that previous photographers hadn't. One look at his photographs of her and people had jumped to conclusions. Their mutual denials had only made the story a hotter item for the gossip columns.

'Now arch your back, honey,' he was saying. 'And open your eyes, just a little. That's it. Perhaps a bit more pout. Yes, like that. Great! Mmm, yes, ve-ry sexy. Yes, hold that!'

The camera clicked away as she held the highly erotic look, and, while common sense told her she was only doing her job, all of a sudden she hated what she did for a living. It was a lie and a con. She didn't feel erotic at that moment. She felt cold and miserable and oddly ashamed.

The old dream she'd once had of becoming a kindergarten teacher came back with a rush. And so did the tears. It was just as well the shoot was over. She scrambled down from the car, wanting nothing more than to get away from here as quickly as possible.

'What's up, honey?' the photographer said kindly as he wrapped a blanket around her. 'Are you sick or something?'

She shook her head in abject misery, swallowing madly as she battled to keep the tears at bay.

'You're tired and cold.' He patted her hand. 'Tomorrow will be better. We're shooting the evening stuff inside the Opera House. Now you go and get changed, then go home and get a good night's sleep. Can't have our beautiful Ebony looking all wan and pasty, can we?'

Ebony was only too glad to escape and hide herself in the caravan. Or she would have been glad . . . if the caravan had been empty.

Alan was sitting on the built-in divan, underneath a window that overlooked the beach and would have given him a clear view of the Porsche.

'So it was *you* watching me!' she accused, her face flaming at the thought that what he'd seen would have only confirmed his opinion of her character. She was a Jezebel, happy to flaunt her body for other men's eyes, turning herself on for the camera as swiftly and easily as she'd always appeared to turn herself on for him.

'Shut the door, Ebony,' he said curtly.

'No. I want you to get out. I told you I don't want to have anything more to do with you, and I meant it. Clear out! Find some other cheap little tart to satisfy your needs, because it's not going to be me!' Too late she realised that sounded as if she categorised herself a cheap little tart as well.

'I don't want some other cheap little tart,' he said, and, unfolding himself, he stood up, striding over to remove her clenched hand from the knob, and shut the door himself. She glared up into his coldly handsome face with its hard blue eyes and thin, cruel lips, then did something she neither planned nor consciously decided to do.

She slapped him, the wild swing of her arm causing the blanket to slip from her shoulders and fall on to the floor. She stood there, half naked, shaking with emotion and trepidation, waiting for Alan to slap her back. Or worse.

But he didn't make a move to touch her, merely arched an eyebrow and absently rubbed the red mark on his cheek. 'I guess I deserved that,' he said, and bent to pick up the blanket.

'W...what?'

'I said I deserved to be slapped.' And he draped the blanket back around her shoulder.

Clutching it to her chest, she frowned up at this strangely meek and mild Alan. He didn't ring true.

'What's going on here?' she demanded agitatedly. 'Is this some new type of game, Alan?'

'Games were never my style, Ebony,' he said drily. 'I learnt them from you.'

A guilty heat zoomed into her face.

Ebony conceded there was a lot of truth in that statement. Not that she'd deliberately set out to turn their affair into a series of dark encounters. She'd reacted badly, however, to Alan's insistence that his relationship with her be a secret. Did he honestly think she hadn't noticed how much he hated himself for wanting her as he did? It had made her perversely determined to make him want her even more. So she'd fulfilled every sexual fantasy a man could ever have. And exulted in every moment of it.

Till afterwards...

Afterwards, she'd always been consumed with shame. It was consuming her now.

'No more, Alan,' she moaned softly. 'No more...' Her head drooped and her shoulders started to shake.

What happened then astounded her.

Alan actually drew her weeping self down on to the divan with him, cradling her gently against his chest and stroking her hair till the sobs subsided.

'There won't be any more,' he said at last. 'I can't take any more either. Let's start again, Ebony. Let's put the past behind us. No more hiding, no more secrets. We'll go out together in public like a normal couple, do things together, go for weekends away together. Would you like that?'

Would she like that? Oh, God...

'You...you want us to be open about our affair?'

'No, I want us to start a new one, a different one.'

'A different one . . .' She blinked several times. 'In what way will it be different?'

'In the ways I've just described. And others. Well, what do you say, Ebony?'

'I don't know *what* to say!'

'I was hoping you'd just say yes. Mother said you would if you loved me as much as she thinks you do.'

Ebony gasped into an upright position, facing Alan with rounded eyes. 'She said that?'

His gaze raked hers. 'Is it true? Do you love me?'

'I . . . I . . .'

He sighed. 'I can empathise with that. It's hard to be sure of one's feelings after the way we've been carrying on.'

'Are . . . are you saying you might be in love with me too?' she asked shakily.

His smile was wry. 'Do you want me to be?'

'Yes,' came her simple but intense reply. 'I've always wanted you to love me.'

He stared over at her, his expression pained. 'You shouldn't say such things when I'm alone with you like this. I promised myself I would be gentler with you this time. Gentler and more considerate and, yes, even romantic, if that would please you. But you make me want to rip that scrap of lace from your body and ravage you right here and now.'

Abruptly, he stood up, his mouth twisting into a cynical and quite sardonic grimace. 'I'm not sure this will work, Ebony. The patterns we've set are very strong. But I'd like to take you somewhere tonight for a long and leisurely dinner, then afterwards I'm going to drive you home where I'm going to try damned hard to keep my hands off you. I want to see if we've got anything going for us other than sex. I want to see if a marriage between us could possibly work.'

'Marriage!' She jumped to her feet.

'You don't want to marry me?' he said, blue eyes narrowing.

'Well, I...I guess I never allowed myself to think you would ever marry *me*. But yes, Alan, yes, I would marry you if you asked me.'

'So you *did* love me all along,' he muttered darkly, his frown an unhappy one.

'I told you I did, Alan. That night in the library...'

His eyes snapped wide. 'But you were little more than a child then, for God's sake. You couldn't have expected me to believe that was for real!'

'I don't think I've ever been a child where you were concerned. I've wanted you from the very first day I saw you.'

'That's ridiculous. You were only fifteen then!'

'Some fifteen-year-old girls are quite old in some regards, Alan.'

His stare showed shock.

A knock on the caravan door interrupted any further conversation. It was one of the crew giving her ten minutes to vacate the caravan. Alan said an abrupt goodbye, saying he had to get back to work and would pick her up at her apartment at eight.

'Wear something modest,' he threw over his shoulder at her as he strode off across the sand.

Ebony did not realise till much later that not once had Alan actually said he loved her.

CHAPTER SEVEN

ALAN parked his white Holden SV5000 outside Ebony's block of flats shortly before eight, but he didn't get out. He sat there for a while, thinking.

Why couldn't he accept that Ebony really truly loved him? His mother insisted she did. Adrianna had suggested the same years ago. Now Ebony herself had said she'd *always* loved him.

Was that the part that bothered him? The 'always' part? Or Ebony's implication that by fifteen she had already been sexually experienced?

If this was so—and her youthful experiences had been pleasurable—then it was possible her concept of love was so entwined with sex and sexual pleasure that she might not be able to separate the two. It troubled Alan, knowing what he knew about Ebony's father. Pierre had been notoriously unfaithful to his wife. Could his daughter be of the same ilk, a compulsive adventurer?

There were some women, Alan imagined, who, because of their make-up, made good mistresses, but awful wives. Their talent for intimacy lay in the bedroom and nowhere else. If they loved, it was not the sort of love that lasted, or could exist without constant physical release.

The image of Ebony spread out on that car this afternoon flashed into his mind, his body remembering the way she'd responded to the intimate gaze of that camera, and the exhorted demands of the man holding it. It made it worse that the photographer was actually one of the endless stream of men she'd reputedly slept with.

How could he not believe the gossip after seeing her in action for himself? The girl was a vamp of the first order, a natural-born siren, unable to stop herself from bewitching every man she came across. His mother was wrong about that. She was not an ill-judged innocent. No way.

But all this rationale counted for nothing when he was with her. This afternoon, when she'd cried once again, he'd wanted nothing but to hold her and comfort her. And it was while he had done so that he had finally come to terms with his love for her.

Which was why he was here now, about to take her to dinner, desperately hoping that a marriage between them would work. Underneath, he doubted it. Ebony might think she wanted to marry him and have children, but he suspected the reality would not please her as much as the idea. He couldn't envisage her wanting that gloriously slender figure of hers swollen out of shape with a baby, or her having to put her own physical pleasure on hold for maybe weeks on end. Neither could he see her giving up her glamorous life as a cover-girl and internationally famous model, any more than he could see himself allowing her to continue her career.

Alan knew his own weaknesses. He was a jealous and possessive man. At least he was where Ebony was concerned. Maybe she had deliberately fuelled his jealousies because of the nature of their relationship, but he knew he wouldn't be able to bear his wife working with all those men she'd already slept with. Neither did he want her flaunting herself in those skimpy outfits she modelled. My God, she might as well have been naked today. He'd been able to see right through that costume.

When his blood began to stir at the visual memory of those hard nipples poking at that black lace, Alan groaned and swiftly alighted from the car, slamming the door in anger at his own lack of control. He'd vowed not to touch her tonight, and just look at him! Damn it, he'd marry her soon, despite his doubts. He'd do anything to have her in his bed every night. He'd even let her go on modelling if he had to. But, by God, he'd get her pregnant as quickly as he could. And then he'd keep her pregnant. She had said she wanted a large family. Well, he'd give her one!

'I like your suit,' was the first thing she said to him on opening her door.

He glanced indifferently down at his clothes. It was just a plain grey suit. Nothing special. Then he looked at her and felt another surge of desire.

Her dress was a simple black wool sheath with long straight sleeves and a not too short skirt. But anything on Ebony looked sexy. His eyes drifted down her long, long legs encased in sheer black stockings till he came to her shiny black patent shoes, their thin ankle straps drawing his attention to her slender ankles and small feet. He recalled how she liked having the soles of those delicate feet massaged, and her toes tickled. And kissed. *And* sucked.

His inward breath was sharp and his eyes jerked upwards. 'Ready to go?' he asked tautly.

'I'll just get my coat and purse.'

The coat was a black and white hound's-tooth jacket, the purse a black clutch in the same patent leather as her shoes.

'You look beautiful,' he said on her return.

'And you look tense,' she returned with a small smile.

His glance was savage for a second, then he too smiled. 'You know me too well. Any chance of skipping dinner?'

'Certainly not!' she reproached. 'And I'm not on the menu for afters, either. I too want to find out if our relationship can survive without sex, Alan. Especially on *your* part.'

He was taken aback. 'Why especially mine?'

'You're the man, after all. Sex is more important to men than women.'

Alan just stopped himself from rolling his eyes at this. If Ebony was anything to go by, then he didn't agree with that statement. Even his own sister had walked out on her toy-boy lover because of sex. The poor devil had finally got off his butt and got himself a job, instead of sponging off Vicki, but unfortunately it was at night. Instead of being proud of him, Vicki was complaining that this would interfere with their love-life! The woman had to be certifiable, but it showed the importance that some females could put on their own satisfaction.

'And another thing I'd like to straighten out, Alan,' Ebony went on firmly. 'You haven't yet said that you love me. Do you or don't you?'

He eyed her closely. 'What answer will get me into your bed later tonight?'

'Neither.'

'OK. Neither.'

It amused him to see her exasperation. Hell, but he wanted to kiss that provocatively pouting mouth!

'Very funny.' She pouted some more.

He suppressed a groan. 'The way I'm feeling to-night isn't funny in the least, but, since you insist, then yes, I love you.'

'You . . . you do?'

There was something enchanting about the way she was looking up at him now, something soft and sweet and vulnerable. Ebony vulnerable he had little experience with, and he warmed to it. Like her tears, it made him want not so much to make love to her, but to simply take her in his arms and reassure her. But he dared not do so in his present state.

His hand reached out to tip her chin up further so that he was looking deep into those beautiful black eyes of hers. 'Yes, I love you. There's no longer any doubt in my mind. I can't say I loved you at fifteen, or even at eighteen, but by the time you were twenty-one I'd fallen in love with you. Is that what you wanted to hear?'

'Yes,' she said, her voice quavering but her eyes glittering with what might have been tears, or triumph. Alan wasn't sure. The latter possibility bothered him for a second, but then she was snaking her long white fingers up around his neck and pulling his mouth to hers, and he didn't care any longer.

A curling sensation contracted his stomach when her tongue sought his, his desire leaping madly. Later, perhaps, he thought, desperately trying to control himself. Later...

His breathing was heavy by the time he pulled away. And so was hers. Her eyes were dilated, and her lips remained tantalisingly parted. I could take her now, he realised. She probably wouldn't stop me, despite her holier-than-thou assertion about not wanting sex for a while.

This realisation had an unnerving and dampening effect on him for once. Ebony as his secret mistress could be as wanton and willing as she liked. The Ebony he loved and wanted to marry was another matter. He would have preferred her to be a little less susceptible to a mere kiss.

'I think we'd better go,' he announced, and abruptly pulled the door shut behind her.

'Where...where are you taking me?' she asked as they made their way down the stairs.

Alan tried not to scowl at her, but, dear lord, even her voice sounded aroused. All breathless and husky and yes...seductive.

'To dinner, of course,' came his curt answer.

'Yes, but what restaurant?'

'Does it matter?'

'No, I suppose not.'

He ground to a halt. Damn it, but he'd see for himself what she was made of, if she had *any* control at all. 'Would you rather we go back upstairs and ring for a pizza?'

He watched her stiffen. 'No, Alan, I don't want to do that. I told you.'

'Just testing. Let's go, then.'

Ebony mulled over Alan's 'just testing' as they drove towards the city. He hadn't been kidding, she realised with some dismay. He *had* been testing her, seeing if a single kiss could change her mind about going back inside.

True, it had been hard to turn him down. She *loved* him. But her desire to forge a real relationship was much stronger than her desire for physical gratification.

Ebony knew, however, that the biggest hurdle to their having a happy life together was Alan's ambivalent feelings about her past behaviour. He had a conservative streak in him that had been seriously challenged by their clandestine and strictly sexual affair. It had troubled him in many ways, not the least of which was that she'd once been his ward, an innocent child whose moral welfare he had been supposed to protect.

Of course, he'd justified it in his mind by thinking of her as a tramp with no morals to speak of. That way, he'd lessened his guilt, but without entirely eliminating it. His opinion of her basic character didn't seem to have changed either, despite his feelings having changed. His lust might have deepened to love, but she was still, in his eyes, a loose woman.

The Alan Carstairs she knew would not marry a loose woman. Certainly not with an easy mind. Ebony believed she had to convince Alan she was nothing of the kind, otherwise any marriage between them was as doomed as their affair had been.

Thinking about marriage and Alan reminded Ebony of her one-time nemesis, Adrianna. Funny, not at any time today had she thought to question Alan over the woman he'd once wanted to marry. But, having thought of her, she could not remain silent.

'What about Adrianna?' she blurted out.

'What about her?'

'Do you still love her?'

Why did he hesitate? Why didn't he just say, No Ebony, how could I love her and love you at the same time?

'No,' he said slowly at long last. 'No, I do not still love Adrianna.'

Ebony frowned. Why didn't his answer satisfy her? Why did she get the feeling he was deceiving her in some way?

'Cross your heart and hope to die?' she challenged with the exuberance of a child.

His laughter was spontaneous and engaging. 'Cross my heart and hope to die.' And he crossed his heart, all the while smiling at her.

Now she felt better, settling back to glance around and see where Alan was heading. Clearly towards the city. 'You still haven't said where you're taking me?' she asked.

'To the Hyatt on the Rocks. Have you been there?'

'No, never. But I've seen it from the harbour. It doesn't look cheap.'

'Are any of the good hotels in Sydney cheap?'

'I don't know. I haven't stayed in any of them. I *live* in Sydney, remember?' Neither have you ever taken me to one of them before, she realised all of a sudden. Either for dinner or anything else. Why had he chosen a hotel? Why not simply a restaurant? Was it because a hotel had rooms for hire?

'I hope you don't think we're going to stay the night,' she said firmly.

'It's not like you to sound so prim and proper.'

'You'd better get used to it,' she countered, a touch sharply.

He slanted her a sceptical look. Ebony's earlier disquiet returned. She'd been right when she'd told Gary she'd created some of her problems herself. She hadn't realised that the day would come when she would desperately want Alan to believe she was a good girl, not a good-time girl.

'I...I'm not sure you have the correct idea about me, Alan,' she tried explaining. 'I'm not in the habit of leaping into bed with every Tom, Dick and Harry, no matter what the tabloids might have implied.'

'Oh?'

'Yes, for your information there's only been one other man beside you.'

'Is that so?'

God, he didn't believe her. She could tell. Should she go on, keep trying to convince him, or let the matter drop?

'Yes, that's so.' She decided to let the matter drop.

Several seconds of electric silence descended.

'Who *was* the other lucky fellow?' Alan finally asked, his voice curiously flat.

Ebony no longer wanted to pursue this conversation. It felt dangerous. She wished she'd never brought the matter up.

'It isn't important,' she mumbled.

'Was it Stevenson?' he demanded, his tone still deadly.

Oh, God...

'I want an answer, Ebony. Was it Stevenson?'

'Yes,' she sighed, and stared out of the passenger window.

'Did you sleep with him over the weekend?'

Her head snapped round. 'Of course not! What do you take me for?'

His eyes were hard as they lanced hers. 'A woman scorned. A woman who likes her sex. A woman who had no idea I loved her. Till today...'

'That's insulting!'

'It's the truth.'

'It's not. You...you don't know the real me.'

'Is that my fault?'

'No,' she sighed again. 'Maybe not...'

Ebony fell silent, her dismay growing. Alan's opinion of her was even darker than she feared. So she was intensely relieved when he said, 'I think it best if we try to forget the past, Ebony. It can't be changed, anyway. Let's concentrate on now, and the future. Surely that's all that matters.'

'I couldn't agree more, Alan,' she agreed eagerly. And flashed him a relieved smile.

His returning look was intense. 'I *do* love you. Too much, perhaps...'

The restaurant he took her to at the Hyatt was called Sevens. It was classy and quiet, with a cosmopolitan menu and an unpretentious but splendid service that would have pleased all but the most snobbish diner. But the most memorable aspect was the view, which would have to be unparalleled throughout the world.

Sydney harbour on a clear and still winter's night was a sight to behold. The inky black waters were a perfect mirror for the lights of the bridge and the surrounding city, the glittering reflections forming a diamond-studded carpet till a passing ferry disturbed the illusion, only to have it return a minute or two later.

'I could sit here and watch the water and the boats all night,' she commented while they waited for their starters to be served. Alan had ordered a white wine—*her* choice—and she was sipping the deliciously chilled liquid with pleasure. 'This is a fairly new hotel, isn't it?'

'Yes, it's only a couple of years old.'

'The site alone must have cost a fortune.' The hotel hugged a small headland that curved around underneath the city-side pylons of the Harbour Bridge. There weren't too many places in Sydney, Ebony appreciated, from which one had an un-impeded view of the harbour and most of its famous surrounds—the Bridge, the Quay, the Rocks, the waterfront and the Opera House.

'I dare say the prices here will reflect that,' Alan said ruefully, 'though the wine list surprises me. Quite reasonable, considering the quality.'

'You're not drinking any of it,' she pointed out.

The corner of his mouth lifted into a ironic half-smile. 'Drinking and going home to an empty bed are not compatible when I'm with you, my love.'

'Oh...' She flushed prettily, her cheeks going quite hot.

Alan frowned, but made no further comment. Silence befell the table. Ebony drank some more wine.

'What shall we talk about?' she asked once the starters had been served. Hers was smoked salmon, Alan's a hot-looking Thai curry.

His laugh carried a dry amusement. 'We're not used to talking much, are we?'

Her hurt look had him apologising.

'Right,' he went on, still with a wry expression on his face. 'Shall we discuss the economy, or the weather, or politics?'

'Tell me how your Man-About-Town stores are going,' she suggested. 'Have they been hit with the recession?'

He shrugged. 'To a degree. But all in all, the tough times have made us more productive and competitive. Once things pick up, we're going to do even better than before. Circumstances have forced me to find more efficient styles and suppliers, and more diverse markets. Would you believe I'm now exporting to Asian markets? That's like taking coals to Newcastle, I know, but there's a demand among wealthy Asians to wear imported garments rather than the locally made articles. Apparently, it's a matter of status. That's why I'm branching out into a designer label, to satisfy those who want to wear original and exclusive designs.'

'Alan, that's marvellous! But then you were always a clever businessman. I know a few womenswear labels who could do with some more progressive thinkers.'

'Do you now?' he smiled.

'I certainly do.'

'Tell me, Ebony, do you like modelling?'

Her disgruntled sigh reflected her recent feelings on the subject. 'I used to, or at least I used to do it without thinking about it too much. It seemed an easy way to make money. And it's always pleasant wearing beautiful clothes. But I'd give it up tomorrow if I could make a living at something else.'

'Or if your husband asked you to?' he said quietly.

She stared at him for a few seconds before realising he was deadly serious. 'Of course,' she said, and could have sworn his whole body shuddered, as though he'd been holding himself very tightly. 'I told you, Alan. I want a large family. When we're married I want to have a baby straight away. If that's all right with you...'

'It's perfectly all right with me.'

His smile was so broad that Ebony almost burst into tears; she'd never felt so happy.

The rest of the meal was eaten in a light, happy mood. They chatted away as they'd never chatted before, sharing amusing incidents in their work lives, teasing each other's tastes in clothes, exchanging opinions on movies they'd seen and places they'd been.

Ebony had never felt so relaxed in Alan's company, yet as the evening drew to a close the desire to have him make love to her was incredibly strong. Maybe because she knew that this time it would be different. This time it would be really making love.

It was Alan, in the end, who pulled back, despite their goodnight kiss having reduced them both to panting, passion-filled messes. When Ebony tried to return to the haven of his arms, he forcibly took her hands and held them away from him.

'Let's see how long we can last,' he suggested huskily. 'Call it a game. A new game.'

Ebony cringed at his use of words. She didn't want there to be any kinds of games between them any more. This was for real, forever. 'And what if I don't like this new game?' she said unhappily.

'It won't last for long, I promise you. But please...humour me in this, Ebony. It's important.'

'How is it important? If you love me and I love you, it's only natural that we'd want to make love. I don't understand you, Alan.'

'Might I remind you of what you yourself said at the beginning of the evening? You wanted to test my love by withholding sex. Maybe I want to do the same with you.'

Her black eyes widened. My God, he actually thought she was some sort of nymphomaniac!

Once again, her behaviour over the past year was coming back to haunt her. What could she do, except go along with him?

'All right, Alan,' she agreed, and, steeling herself, reached up to give him a chaste peck on the cheek. 'We'll wait.'

He seemed pleased. 'That's my girl.'

Ebony went to bed that night telling herself that if she was patient and understanding everything would turn out all right. After all, she had much to be grateful for. Alan didn't love Adrianna any more. He loved *her*. And he wanted to marry her and have babies with her. That was much much more than she'd ever hoped for.

Why, then, as she lay in her cold, lonely bed, was she so worried? Why did she keep thinking that she was fighting a losing battle, trying to gain Alan's trust and respect?

Her final thought before she drifted off to sleep was not quite so pessimistic. It brought a groan, however. Gary was going to kill her when she told him she'd changed her mind again!

CHAPTER EIGHT

As IT turned out, Ebony didn't get the opportunity to speak personally to Gary over the next few days. Work took up all Tuesday, Wednesday and Thursday during the daytime, and going out with Alan occupied every evening till nearly midnight. Gary left a message on her answering machine on the Wednesday, complaining that she was never home and that he would leave it up to her to contact him, otherwise he would expect her to arrive at his hotel room around seven on Friday evening.

When Ebony did try to contact him at the Ramada, he wasn't in, so she left a message to say she would see him precisely at seven p.m. on the Friday. She felt bad enough that he had made all those arrangements for nothing, and decided the least she could do was give him her news first-hand, then have a farewell dinner with him.

Of course, there was no question of telling Alan any of this; she was not a fool. But that left the problem of inventing some excuse not to see him on the Friday evening. The matter was beginning to cause her some stress when Alan himself, towards the end of their date on the Thursday night, provided the perfect solution.

They'd been out to dinner and a show, one of those modern psychological plays which she'd never liked and didn't appreciate. She'd run out of discussion about it on the way home when Alan had turned to her and said, 'By the way, I can't take you out tomorrow night. I have a business dinner which I just can't get out of. Sorry.'

She hoped she had hidden her relief. 'It's all right. I understand.'

'You don't mind?'

'Of course not. My hair's overdue for a treatment and that takes hours, anyway,' she said without any real guilt. Everyone told little white lies to shield the ones they loved from hurt and worry.

Actually, Ebony was relieved about Friday night for more reasons than her dinner date with Gary. Platonic-style outings with Alan had gradually proved to be more of a trial than the wonderfully sweet and romantic encounters she had hoped they might be. The physical attraction between them was so strong that continually denying its natural conclusion became a barrier to other forms of communication. Their conversation had become stilted and forced, their goodnight kisses nothing more than fleeting pecks. On these occasions, she longed to throw her arms around Alan, kiss him properly then drag him inside.

Suppressing a sigh, she was off in another world till she found herself opening her front door, Alan standing at her shoulder.

'You were very quiet in the car,' he said. 'Are you annoyed with me because I can't take you out tomorrow night?'

She turned to lift startled eyes to his. 'No, of course not. Why should I be?'

He shrugged, but his eyes were troubled. His concern touched her. Laying an understanding hand on his cheek, she smiled softly. 'Don't be silly, Alan. I know you're a busy man.'

His hand covered hers and Ebony immediately tensed. 'I love you,' he said. 'You know that, don't you?'

'Yes,' she choked out. Dear God, just go. I can't take much more of this.

But already his mouth was bending and this time his goodnight kiss in no way resembled a peck. Ebony gave a soft groan as his lips flowered open over hers, his probing tongue-tip inviting her to part her lips as well.

No invitation was required. She was already ahead of him, sending her own tongue forward to meet his. The hand on his cheek slid around his neck, her other hand coming to rest on his chest. She could feel his heart beating madly underneath the heat of her palm. His kiss grew fierce and his arms swept her hard against him.

When he broke from her mouth he was literally shaking. 'No,' he astonished her by saying. 'No...'

'But why not?' she protested, half in shock, half in frustration. Dear lord, but she wanted him, and he wanted her. Why should they keep on torturing themselves like this? 'This is crazy, Alan,' she muttered.

His sigh was ragged. 'It's something I have to do.'

'But *why*? We're just not cut out for this kind of relationship, Alan. It's unnatural.'

'There has to be more to a marriage than just sex,' he said firmly. 'If we can't go one single week without it, then what kind of people are we?'

Such thinking fired her very Gallic temper. 'I'll tell you what kind of people we are. We're a man and woman very much in love with each other. And we're not married yet, might I remind you! What further tests will you come up with before we are, I wonder? Oh, go home to bed, Alan,' she threw at him. 'As for myself, I think I'll go inside and drink a whole bottle of wine all by myself. Maybe then I'll be able to forget that the man I love doesn't want to make love to me any more!' And with that, she slammed the door in his face and locked it.

Shock galvanised Alan to the spot for a couple of seconds. Then an answering anger took over. His closed fists lifted to bang on her door, but he stopped himself just in time. Damn it, but she was right, wasn't she? He knew she was right. What had seemed like a good idea at the time had just not worked out. So their love was mainly physical at this point in time. So what? Ebony's intense sexuality was one of the things he loved about her. It fired a passion in him he'd never thought he possessed, made him feel like a man in the most basic and satisfying way.

It was one thing to know how to make love to a woman—something he prided himself on being able to do well—but there was nothing to compare with the woman you loved showing an overwhelming amount of pleasure in your arms, in listening to her unrestrained sounds of satisfaction, in being on the receiving end of such uninhibited and passionate loving.

He ached at this very moment to have those sensuous lips of hers rove all over him. God, the thought of the sensations she could evoke was sending the blood surging along his veins, making his flesh swell even further than it already had.

The temptation to thump on that door was powerful. But there was a stronger force. Pride, probably. Certainly not any notion of testing. He could no longer cling to the hope that this last week of denial had proved a thing. It had, as Ebony had pointed out, been a disaster, not one moment going by when he hadn't wanted to pick her up and take her off somewhere private where he could make mad passionate love to her. To be honest, it had seemed to focus their relationship more on sex than ever before.

The human being was a contrary animal, he realised testily. Forbid it something, and suddenly that thing became even more attractive and imperative than before.

Alan shook his head, turned and walked slowly down the stairs, each step an agony. He would call her in the morning, apologise, then ask her to spend the weekend with him. Maybe he would take her out on his boat; she'd always liked that as a young girl. And being on the water was both private and relaxing. He would cruise up to Broken Bay, and find a secluded cove to drop anchor in. He'd ask her to bring that black costume she'd modelled the other day. Not that he planned on having her swim in it. He didn't plan on her having it on for long at all ...

Alan's smile was sardonic as he let himself into his car. This was familiar territory, he realised, though he found a certain irritation in his letting her slip back into the role of mistress in his mind. But damn it all, he just couldn't wait!

It was seven forty-five on the Friday evening, and Alan had been sitting at the cocktail bar in the dimly lit restaurant for several minutes, his dry Martini down to the olive.

Adrianna was late. When she'd contacted him earlier in the week, saying she was coming to Sydney for business and a pre-natal check-up, and expressing a wish to see him while she was in town, he hadn't been able to turn her down. Yet he'd felt vaguely guilty about it, especially when he'd lied to Ebony. He'd felt even guiltier when Ebony had been so trusting, accepting what he told her without even asking a single question. If *she'd* begged off a date with him, saying she had a business dinner, he'd probably have given her the third degree.

Ebony would not be pleased, however, if she found out who Alan's 'business' dinner was with. But there was no reason why she should find out. This place was out of the way and not popular with celebrities or people from the fashion world. He glanced around again to make sure. Nope. No one he knew. Darn it, where *was* that woman?

She breezed in a couple of minutes later, looking as elegant and coolly beautiful as only Adrianna could look at six months pregnant.

'Am I terribly late?' she exclaimed, a cloud of flowery perfume assailing his nostrils as she leant forward to kiss him on the cheek. She hoisted herself on to the stool next to him, her cleverly layered outfit in cream wool hiding her pregnancy completely.

'A Perrier, please,' she told the barman before turning towards Alan. 'The gynaecologist was running late and then my taxi got stuck in some traffic and in the end I jumped out and walked. Am I forgiven?' She pushed back her curtain of sleek blonde hair and flashed him a winning smile.

He smiled back. Just. Oh, Adrianna, he thought. If only I could have fallen in love with you all those years ago, things would have been much simpler.

She gave him a sharp look. 'That's not much of a smile. And you're looking terribly tired. Are you working too hard?'

'Probably.'

'Alan, you bad man. You need someone to take you in hand.'

'I couldn't agree more,' he said blackly.

Her lovely grey eyes widened slightly. She picked up the glass of mineral water and took a sip. 'That doesn't sound like you,' she said. 'The Alan Carstairs I used to know and love was always in control of his own life.'

'You never loved me, Adrianna, more's the pity.'

Her hand covered his where it was resting on the bar. 'That's not true, Alan. I did love you. You were a good friend, and a damned good lover. I still love you. But I'm *in love* with Bryce. There's a difference.'

'Mmm.'

Her laughter was light and teasing. 'Now what does "mmm" mean?'

'Nothing.' He looked over at her, schooling his face into a less troubled expression. The woman was too damned intuitive. 'So tell me, Adrianna, what did you want to see me about?'

'Shall we go to our table first? I could take this with me and you could order yourself a nice bottle of red. A full-blooded claret might cheer you up.'

'No more hedging, Adrianna,' he began again once they were settled at a table in the corner. 'What's up?'

'Nothing, really. I've been thinking a lot about you lately and I had to come to Sydney anyway to have an ultrasound, so I decided to kill two birds with one stone.' She drew in then exhaled a deep breath. 'You'll probably think I'm prying, but I wanted to find out what happened between you and Ebony. Four years ago when you came to my wedding I could have sworn she was as much in love with you as you were with her. No, don't deny it again, Alan. I won't ever believe it was only lust you felt for the girl, despite her tender age. You're just not the type. I've been half expecting to get an invitation to *your* wedding all this time, but it never came...'

Alan clenched his teeth hard in his jaw. He didn't want to play true confessions with Adrianna about Ebony. He wasn't in the mood for a lecture. And Adrianna would give him one if she knew what had been going on this past year. God, yes, she'd really give him a tongue-lashing.

Adrianna was not forgiving when it came to any form of chauvinistic treatment of women. A staunchly independent career woman, she had made some astonishing compromises to marry Bryce McLean. But one could only admire both the woman and her cattle-station-owner husband for the depth of their feelings for each other. It was the type of love that could move mountains.

'Ebony and I did fall out with each other for a few years,' he admitted, thinking what an understatement that was! 'But we go out together occasionally now.'

'And?' Adrianna probed.

Alan shrugged. 'She had a lot of growing up to do, Adrianna. I didn't want to rush her.'

'Well, she's certainly all grown-up now, and so beautiful it's just criminal. Would you believe I saw her tonight?'

Alan tried very hard to look nonchalant, but every nerve in his body had snapped tight. 'You saw her? Where?'

'She was going into one of the hotel lifts as I was coming out. I went to call out to her, but the doors shut and she was gone. I don't think she saw me.'

Alan tried to stop the black suspicions from crowding in. 'Are you sure it was Ebony?' he asked casually.

'Of course I'm sure. How many girls look like Ebony? You know, it's not surprising she's become a highly sought-after model with that face and figure, not to mention that hair! I tried to sign her up for one of my fashion shows not long ago, but she only models black, it seems, and I don't design in black.'

'Yes,' Alan said on automaton. 'But it's worked surprisingly well for her, that black-only business. Still, I think she'd have been successful anyway.'

Adrianna gave him an exasperated glance. 'So when are you going to snap her up, Alan? A girl like that must have plenty of admirers. You wouldn't want to wait too long.'

'I won't,' he said with more feeling than he'd intended.

Adrianna looked surprised. 'That's more like it. Now tell me, how's *your* business going? Better than mine, I hope.'

Alan let the whole meal go by before he was able to ask the one question that was gnawing a jagged hole into his insides. 'I'll take you back to your hotel, Adrianna,' he said as he helped her into her coat. 'Which one are you staying at, by the way?'

She smiled at him over her shoulder. 'The Ramada.'

They arrived back at the hotel by ten—Adrianna had not wanted a late evening. Alan ushered her across the foyer, his emotional state something like a kamikaze pilot. He didn't care if he ran into Ebony. He didn't care if *she* saw *him* with Adrianna. He felt homicidal and suicidal at the one time.

But as fate would have it, nobody ran into anybody else. He delivered Adrianna to her room, kissed her goodnight, and returned to the foyer. On approaching Reception, he asked for Gary Stevenson's room number, vainly hoping that they would tell him he'd checked out days ago.

But he was there all right.

When he asked to be connected by telephone he was told that Mr Stevenson wanted all calls held that evening, but he could leave a message if he liked.

Alan shook his head and turned away from the desk, feeling sick. He went outside into the street and simply walked. After an hour of mindless pacing, he found a telephone and rang Ebony's apartment, holding his breath till it clicked over to her answering machine. He knew from experience that meant she wasn't home. She didn't use the answering machine while she was merely asleep. He hung up and went back to the hotel, finding an unobtrusive spot in the foyer where he could sit and watch the lifts without being seen himself.

By eleven-thirty, he was beginning to think he was crazy, sitting there. Then he saw her coming out of the lift with a leanly built, fairish man whom he immediately recognised. Stevenson had once done a fashion shoot for his Man-About-Town label many years ago. He'd been a womaniser back then. Nothing had changed, apparently.

Alan watched, seething, while Gary placed his hands on Ebony's shoulders and kissed her. OK, so it wasn't a long kiss, but it wasn't a peck either. He saw Ebony wag a finger at him and laugh. But then she went up on tiptoe and kissed him back on the cheek.

Alan ground his teeth, forcing himself to stay right where he was till Stevenson turned to walk back to the lifts and Ebony hurried away. For a few terrible moments he battled with the temptation to go over and mash the bastard to a pulp. But he didn't. He knew who was to blame for what had happened tonight. And it wasn't Gary Stevenson.

A blackness enveloped Alan, a blackness full of jealousy and fury and revenge. She would never do this to him again, he vowed savagely. Never!

CHAPTER NINE

FROM the moment Alan picked Ebony up early on the Saturday morning, she felt something was wrong. Why she should feel that, she had no idea, for Alan was, if anything, extra attentive, a ready smile coming to his face whenever she glanced his way. It almost seemed as if he was trying to hide something, though she could not, for the life of her, imagine what it could be.

'Did your—er—business dinner go all right?' she asked on the drive to his place.

Was she imagining things or did he tense slightly at her question? His mouth was smiling when he looked over at her, but not his eyes.

'Excellent,' he pronounced. 'Most productive and informative.'

'In what way?'

'Pardon?'

'In what way was it productive and informative?'

He gave her another of those unnervingly cold smiles. 'Must you bother your pretty little head about business today? Now that I've put aside all that nonsense about our not indulging ourselves, I'd like you to concentrate on only one subject. *Me*.'

Ebony stared at him. When he'd called and asked her to spend the weekend with him on his boat, she'd assumed they would start making love again.

The prospect had both relieved and excited her. Now, however, she felt oddly chilled. Alan's mood seemed dark, even darker than it had ever been when they'd been conducting their love-hate affair.

'Have I said something wrong?' he asked silkily. 'Am I to take it that you're no longer as anxious to have me in your bed as you were the other night?'

Ebony gulped. Suddenly, she didn't know what to say, or how to answer that two-edged question. If she said yes, then she would sound sex-mad. If she said no, then he would think she was a tease and a hypocrite. God, what was the matter with Alan today? Why did she get the feeling he wanted her to feel awful?

'I . . . I haven't changed my mind about what I said the other night,' she tried. 'I think when two adults are in love, then making love is the most natural, beautiful thing in the world. I don't find my wanting you to make love to me a thing to be ashamed of, Alan.'

'I can only applaud such fine sentiments. But what if you *weren't* in love with me? Would you still be prepared to go to bed with me?'

'But I *do* love you. Oh, Alan, is that what's bothering you today? Are you beginning to doubt my love again?'

He looked taken aback. 'Why do you think something's wrong with me today? I've been perfectly normal.'

She laughed. 'You have to be joking! You're wound up tight as a drum, and you keep smiling at me with about as much warmth as the wicked old witch in Hänsel and Gretel.'

'I see ... Is this better?' He flashed her a smile that was marginally improved, if one ignored the new overtones of the big bad wolf in Little Red Ridinghood. But Ebony decided not to mention that. Maybe he was just as frustrated as she was, but it was coming out a different way.

'What have you told your mother about us?' she asked, believing a change of subject was called for.

'That we're going steady, view matrimony.'

She laughed. 'What a quaint term! ''Going steady''. Oh, Alan, you're so old-fashioned in some ways.'

'Am I? Well, that's too bad because I'm not going to change. I happen to believe in old-fashioned values like loyalty and fidelity.'

'I should hope so! I wouldn't want my man straying all over the place like a ... a ...'

'Man-About-Town?' he suggested drily.

She pulled a face at him. 'I was going to say alley-cat.'

'Alley-cat's a female term. Women are called alley-cats.'

'Miaow!' she mouthed, and clawed her hands like a cat. 'Now tell me what your mother said about us or I'll scratch your eyes out.'

'What a good idea,' he muttered. 'Then I wouldn't be able to see any more evil.'

Ebony gave an exasperated sigh as her hands dropped back into her lap. 'Are you trying to avoid answering my questions? I'm not sure you've told your mother about us at all.'

'I have. Unfortunately...'

She was taken aback. 'Why "unfortunately"?'

Alan shrugged. 'You know what she's like—runs off at the mouth—though actually she was struck dumb for a moment or two. But when she did find her voice, everything she said was complimentary. She thinks you're a cross between a martyr and a saint for loving me after the way I've treated you.'

Ebony frowned. 'You mean you're still taking all the blame? You didn't say anything about how I treated you?'

His sideways glance was sharp. 'Are you confessing to treating me badly, Ebony?'

'Well, I...I did let you think things that weren't true, and I...I...oh, you know how rotten I was at times. I got some weird kind of pleasure out of making you jealous. I feel quite ashamed when I think about it now.'

'You mean you wouldn't deliberately try to make me jealous any more?'

'Good lord, no, I'd go to great lengths to avoid it. Your jealousy can be quite frightening at times, you know.'

'Can it, now? I think I like the sound of that. Ah...here we are.' He pulled into the driveway, braking while he used the remote control to open the high iron gates that guarded the Carstairses' home. 'I hope you brought that sexy black costume as I asked you to. I've a mind to see you in it.'

And out of it, you lying, treacherous bitch, he thought savagely as he shot the car inside, crunching to a halt beside the front porch. Not a trace of guilt all morning, he noted bitterly. But that was only to be expected. She had no conscience. None at all. She'd been frustrated by the events of the week and had taken the first opportunity to have her insatiable needs satisfied, turning to one of her old flames, someone who would know exactly the sort of wild lovemaking she liked.

The thought of what had gone on in that hotel room last night reinforced his dark resolve to carry through with his revenge. Women like her had to be punished. They could not be allowed to toy with a decent man's feelings. She thought she had his measure, did she? She thought she could marry him, take his money and his love, then sneak around behind his back, screwing whomever she pleased.

When he thought of how she'd fooled him with her tears and her protestations of love . . .

But he would have the last laugh. He'd take the only thing she had to offer a man, take it and take it and take it over the next two days. And when he'd finally sated his lust—for that was all that was left of his feelings—then he would toss her aside like the disgustingly used creature she was.

'There's your mother coming out to meet us,' Ebony was saying.

Deirdre Carstairs had eagerly awaited their arrival, and, hearing Alan's car on the gravel, had dashed out of the front door.

Ebony opened the car door and jumped out to meet her. They hugged each other delightedly.

'Ebony! Darling!' Deirdre gushed, and held her away to look at her with love and satisfaction. 'Oh, I'm so happy. You and Alan! Who would have believed it? You did say you wanted a large family, didn't you?' she went on exuberantly while Alan busied himself taking Ebony's overnight bag from the boot.

'Alan,' she called over to him. 'Ebony hasn't a ring yet. Oh, and we should have an engagement party. Yes, that's what we should do. Vicki can help me. She's good at throwing parties. You can leave the ring till then, I suppose.'

'Thank you for your kind permission,' Alan said curtly, guilt assailing him at his mother having to be hurt by all this. He'd been premature in telling her about his new relationship with Ebony. Premature and bloody stupid. All he could do now was try to minimise future hurts and embarrassments.

'Would you be offended if I begged off the engagement party for a while?' he said on joining them on the front doorstep. 'Ebony and I have only just discovered each other, so to speak, and we'd like some more time to ourselves. You must realise she's a celebrity in this city. Her engagement to her guardian would make good copy for the tabloids, and maybe not all of it so good. You get my drift?'

Deirdre frowned. 'I hadn't thought of that. But you're right. They could put a nasty slant on it.'

'You haven't mentioned anything to Vicki as yet, have you?'

'No, I haven't heard hide nor hair of my darling daughter since she scooted out of here last Sunday.'

'Then don't. I'll tell her myself, eventually. OK?'

'I suppose so,' his mother sighed, then shrugged. 'Well, come on inside. Bob's packed a special picnic basket for you to take on the boat. Nothing's too much trouble for his "Mr Alan". And before you ask me if I've told him about you two, then the answer is yes. I'll just have to swear him and Bill to secrecy.'

'I'm not so worried about Bob and Bill,' Alan muttered. 'They aren't big-mouths like Vicki.'

'Speaking of Vicki,' Ebony piped up once they'd moved inside, 'did she patch things up with her boyfriend?'

Deirdre threw her an astonished glance. 'Didn't Alan tell you? He gave Alistair a job in the main factory as assistant to one of the designers—a day shift, of course—so that Vicki's problem was miraculously solved. Wasn't that sweet of him?'

Alan retreated from the admiration in those black eyes as they turned towards him. He didn't want Ebony to admire him. Certainly not today.

'Your son pretends to be tough, Mrs Carstairs,' she said warmly, 'but he's a real softie, do you know that?' She reached out to lay a tender hand on his forearm.

Alan felt an electric shiver run right through him. Damn her, he thought. Only a light touch and a melting look, and his desire for revenge was weakening. She was like a drug, all of her. Not just her sexuality, but her whole personality. God, but he still loved her despite everything. Still loved and wanted her.

But how could he turn a blind eye to betrayals such as were perpetrated in that hotel room last night? What would happen the next time she was denied sex for a while? Hell, he'd never be able to trust her out of his sight for a moment.

On the other hand, if he didn't marry Ebony, he would never marry anyone, never have children, never give his mother the grandchildren she so longed for. She loved Ebony like a daughter and would continue to love her without reservation, provided he never enlightened her of Ebony's failings. The girl was not all bad, having but the one fatal flaw in her character: she had no conscience about sex.

Could such a marriage work? he agonised. Was he strong enough, bold enough, forgiving enough to take on such a woman?

That was the dilemma facing him. Yet when he looked deeply into her eyes as he was at this moment, there didn't seem to be any dilemma. Her gaze was truly loving, and oddly innocent. Maybe she didn't realise how wrong her behaviour was. Maybe, in her mind, sex and love were two entirely different things.

Her father had been like that. Pierre had seemed to love his wife, yet that hadn't stopped him seducing every pretty girl who came his way. Judith had done her best to keep her husband faithful, always travelling with him wherever he went, but Pierre was incorrigible. He often boasted to Alan that he only needed an hour here and there to accomplish his adulterous adventures. There were some women, he'd claimed, who liked to be treated as sex objects. They enjoyed strictly sexual encounters, the risk of discovery increasing their passion and pleasure.

Alan had not agreed with him. Till now...

Suddenly, his mind was made up, his insides tightening with the acceptance of what he was going to do.

'Being a softie is not always a good thing for a man to be,' he told Ebony brusquely. 'I won't be letting it become a habit. Shall we move along now? I'd like to reach our destination while the sun's still high in the sky and has some warmth in it.'

Ebony thoroughly enjoyed the cruise through the heads of Sydney Harbour and up the coast, loving the feel of the sea breeze and the salt spray in her face. Alan had occasionally taken her out like this when she'd been home on holidays from boarding-school, and they had been outings she'd treasured. Usually it had been in the summer, and she'd loved to watch him move around the boat dressed in shorts and little else. She'd been very aware of him as a man even then, loving the look of his lean male body and dreaming what it would be like to touch it, kiss it.

Her heart squeezed tight and she gripped the railing harder. Alan's body had turned out to be every bit as good as she'd originally fantasised. She'd adored the feel of the steely muscles in his flat stomach, the broad shoulders and hair-roughened chest, the taut buttocks and powerful thighs.

But today... today it would be even better, because it would not only be the body of the man she loved, but the body of the man who loved her. God, but she'd waited a lifetime for that kind of lovemaking.

A shiver of anticipation ran through her and she turned to glance back at Alan, her hair whipping across her face as she did so. He was in the cabin behind the wheel, his dark good looks and tanned skin enhanced by the white shorts and open-weaved white top he was wearing.

Sweeping her hair off her mouth, she went to smile at him. But the smile died before it was born once she saw the way Alan was looking at her. No, *staring* at her. The wind was lifting the beach-coat away from her thighs and buttocks, revealing the high-cut black lace swimming costume Alan had asked her to put on before leaving Double Bay. His gaze was riveted to the revealing costume and the flesh therein, and it didn't look like a loving gaze to her eyes. It was the same way Alan had often looked at her since they'd become lovers—with a combination of lust and contempt.

Shock turned her mind off the necessity to keep a firm hold on the railing, and when the nose of the boat crashed into the top of a wave Ebony lurched sideways, almost losing her balance.

'Hey, watch it!' Alan yelled out to her, his face flashing true alarm. His instant and very real concern brought some soothing to the sickening suspicion that he'd lied about loving her.

But she was not entirely soothed. There remained an apprehensive niggle of doubt, her mind racing to find evidence to support or tear down such a destructive fear.

Alan *had* been very quiet on the trip up. More than quiet. Almost morose. She'd thought he was concentrating on the wheel, but perhaps there was another, darker explanation. Maybe he was feeling guilty at having deceived her. Or maybe he wasn't...

'You'd better go round the back of the boat, Ebony,' he ordered brusquely. 'You almost gave me a heart attack just then. You're usually more sure-footed than that.'

Ebony made her way carefully round to the back of the boat where the sunken decking was a lot safer, but she could not dispel the disquiet in her heart. She tried telling herself she was being neurotic, even paranoid. Of course Alan loved her. Men did not marry these days just for sex.

But he hasn't married you yet, came the insidious thought. He doesn't even want an engagement party. Maybe he'll never marry you...

Ebony turned to frown at Alan, whose back was to her now. He'd been behaving strangely from the moment he'd picked her up, hadn't he?

Suddenly, his head jerked round to find her frowning at him.

'You all right back there?' he asked.

'I . . . I suppose so.'

'Not seasick, are you? You look a bit off.'

'Maybe a little.'

'You'll be OK in a minute. The sea's behind us now. Only still water ahead.'

When she looked back at the water Ebony saw they were well into the mouth of the Hawkesbury river and the water was indeed calm. Not so her insides.

Taking a deep, steadying breath, she let it out slowly, finally convincing herself she was imagining things. Life had been rotten for so long that she'd lost the knack of being happy, of accepting that dreams could come true. She clung to the fact that Alan was basically a good man who would never deliberately deceive anyone. Their affair had been twisted by unusual circumstances, but now that everything was all out in the open there was no reason to feel this insane fear. No reason at all.

Ebony sighed again, forced a smile to her lips, and determined to be happy.

The river, she noted, was quite crowded with a plethora of pleasure craft, all out for a day on the water. The lack of wind plus an unseasonable warmth made for very pleasant conditions for fishing or cruising or just lying in the sun, enjoying being alive. Ebony was finally relaxing, watching the water and the other boats go by, when Alan suddenly veered right and headed up a narrow and rather out-of-the way branch of the river.

An immediate tension gripped which showed she hadn't totally dispelled her earlier irrational unease.

For why should she worry if Alan was looking for a private spot where they could be together without being observed? It wasn't beyond the realms of possibility that they might like to move around the boat *au naturel*. Ebony was not shy about her body and she knew Alan liked to see her that way.

Now stop being ridiculous, she told herself impatiently. This was getting beyond a joke.

They dropped anchor shortly after noon in a small, almost hidden cove.

'What an isolated spot,' Ebony remarked, trying to sound relaxed as she glanced around the secluded area.

But she wasn't relaxed. The lack of other boats around, plus the unearthly silence, was unnerving her. Neither did she like the look of the thick virgin bush that came right down to the water's edge, or the dark jagged rocks that lined the shore. Even the water looked forbidding, cold and deep and ominous-looking. One could easily imagine monsters lurking in those dark green depths, waiting to entwine their tentacles around the legs of anyone foolish enough to challenge their territory.

A dark shiver reverberated all the way down her spine.

'You can't possibly be cold.'

Ebony was startled by Alan's sudden appearance behind her, his hands on her shoulders firm and almost imprisoning.

'Feeling better now?' he went on, his voice husky in her ear, his hands undoing the buttons of the

thigh-length black and white striped beach-coat. In
no time the garment was being parted by Alan's
nimble fingers, and Ebony's pulse-rate was starting
to escalate. But so was an accompanying underlying feeling of panic.

Surely he didn't mean to have her right here and
now? She'd envisaged a romantic picnic lunch, a
bottle of wine, a long and tender foreplay.

The coat had been discarded and already his
hands were roving hotly over her body. Already it
was responding. Dear God, it knew nothing else,
after all, nothing but a wild succession of harsh
and impassioned possessions. Never for her a tender
or loving union. Never...

A tortured moan escaped her lips when she felt
her breasts swelling, felt their erect nipples poking
at the confining lace. And then his hands were
sweeping back down the length of her body and he
was whispering wicked words in her ears, words
that should have disgusted her, but didn't. Was she
past disgust? Past everything except the need to
have his body blended with hers?

Apparently so...

Closing her eyes, she leant back against Alan's
body, giving herself up to whatever he wanted. She
felt utterly boneless and without will. She felt dazed.

'You're still mine, aren't you?' Alan rasped, his
hands skimming the front of the costume, making
her shudder as they brushed over those hardened
peaks before travelling further down her body. He
caressed the smooth white skin of her quivering
thighs, first down the outside of her legs then the

inside. His fashion-experienced mind quickly discovered the easy velcro opening, and he gave a growl of satisfaction as he gained easy access to the moist flesh within.

Ebony shuddered again, then lay her head back against his shoulder and squeezed her eyes even more tightly shut. 'You must stop,' she groaned after a couple of minutes' exquisite torture.

'Must I? Ah, yes... You want the real thing, *need* the real thing. Nothing else will do for my lovely Ebony.' His hands had stopped their intimate exploration of her flesh, to her intense relief. She could barely think. Now, perhaps, he would turn her round, kiss her, make proper and beautiful love to her.

Instead, he wrapped a strong arm around her waist, holding her captive while there was the rustle of clothes being removed close behind her. And then he was taking her hands and curling them over the top rail, easing her hips backwards, spreading her legs.

There was a moment of confusion at the choosing of a position that prevented any real sense of intimacy. But it was hard to think clearly when one was already on the edge, when every nerve-ending was twisted tight in anticipation of becoming one flesh with the man she loved.

It wasn't till Alan pushed the costume up to her waist with shaking hands that her confusion crystallised into dismay, and she saw this encounter for what it was: nothing different from all their previous encounters.

But already he was inside her, already taking her along that path he'd taken her so many times before.

Her dismay sharpened. This was not what she wanted any more, or what she'd believed this weekend would be like. She'd thought they would make love—*really* make love.

There was no doubt about it any more. Alan didn't really love her.

So why was she letting him do this to her? Ebony agonised. Why was she gripping this railing with a white-knuckled intensity, hating it yet wanting him to keep going, to plunge deeper and harder till she was beyond thought, beyond hating herself for being no more than a faceless receptacle for Alan's lust?

Stop him, her pride demanded. For pity's sake, stop him . . .

It wasn't till she saw her tortured reflection in the water below that her body listened to her brain, her arousal going as quickly as it had come. Alan must have sensed her emotional withdrawal for he stopped abruptly to pull her upright, holding her tightly against him, their bodies still one. His breathing was heavy and hoarse in her ear.

'You're not with me, are you?' he rasped into her ear, his voice shaking. 'Why, Ebony? This is what you usually like, what you've often craved, this type of sex. Tell me what it is that makes you so lacking in fire today,' he taunted. 'Normally you'd have been over the edge by now. Tell me what's wrong. Are you a little tired, perhaps?'

'No...I...' A sob caught in her throat. 'Oh, please. I...I don't want it like this any more...'

But when she struggled to escape, he scooped her back against him with ruthless ease. She'd always known he was physically strong, but it wasn't till this moment that she had seriously been afraid of his dominant male strength. She was no match for him out here, and there was no use screaming. All she had as a defence was her mind, and his conscience.

'I...I thought you loved me,' she said broken-heartedly.

'I do.'

'But this isn't making love,' she sobbed.

'Isn't it? Well, we can't have that, can we? How about this, then? Is this better?'

'Oh, God,' she whimpered when he began to caress her again, gently now, despite the other arm wrapped around her waist being as iron-like as ever. And while there was something horribly false about his tender touch, it was also insidiously seductive. God, why did he have to know her body so well? It wasn't fair...

'Yes,' he urged thickly when she shuddered with involuntary pleasure. 'Yes...'

The arm around her waist loosened to find its way up to her breasts and she found herself being bombarded with even more sensations. Nipples were teased till they were tense and aching. All of her was tense and aching. By now all she wanted was for Alan to bend her to that railing once more, to do whatever he wanted, to give her body the release it craved, his oddly derisive tone of a few moments ago quite forgotten.

Till he spoke to her like that again.

'I knew you wouldn't be able to resist for long,' he jeered.

Alan's obvious contempt cut through the fog of arousal that had been blanketing Ebony's pride, forcing her to face the unfaceable once more. He *didn't* love her. His offer of marriage was a sham, and so was this weekend. He'd tricked her into giving him the only thing he'd ever wanted from her, into resuming her old role as mistress.

The hurt was unbearable, the pain infusing her limbs with a crazed strength. With one almighty heave, she ejected Alan from her body, sending him sprawling back on to the deck. Then, without even turning around, she climbed up on to the railing and dived into the murky depths of the river.

CHAPTER TEN

EBONY was not the best swimmer in the world, but adrenalin and the freezing water had her striking out with frenzied strokes for the shore. Not for a second did she turn round to see if Alan had followed her, though she thought she heard a loud splash a few seconds later. This only served to make her swim harder and faster.

She made it to the shore without being overtaken and was trying to find a foothold on the slippery rocks when pain sliced through the ball of her foot, making her cry out in agony. Instinctively, she tried to lift her foot up to see what had happened, the action making her slide back out into the deeper water, and it was then that Alan caught her.

This time she fought him with every ounce of energy she had, thrashing about in the water, slapping, kicking and struggling till she was weak with exhaustion.

'Let me go,' she cried wearily when he scooped an arm around her waist and lay her on her back, life-saver-wise, dragging her slowly back towards the boat.

'To go where?' he snarled. 'Into that bush? Don't be ridiculous, Ebony. Now be quiet till I get you back on board. You might want to kill yourself, but I have no such wish.'

It was quite an effort to get aboard, but they
finally made it, Ebony collapsing on the deck into
a bedraggled heap, her chest heaving, her long hair
plastered down her back. For a few seconds she lay
there with her eyes shut, too tired to do anything
about the black lace costume which had ridden right
up under her bust.

When she opened her eyes it was to find Alan
nowhere in sight. Not that this made her contemplate another crazy escape attempt. There was nowhere to escape to, she realised wretchedly. She was
here till Alan decided to take her home.

Shivering now, she levered herself up into a sitting
position and pulled the costume down into place.
It was then that she saw the trail of blood on the
deck, and remembered the incident in the water.

Slowly widening eyes surveyed the bottom of her
foot and the fresh blood bubbling from it. She
stared at the blood for what seemed like ages before
the oddest feeling came over her. Having never
fainted before in her life, Ebony didn't recognise
the warning signs, so a few seconds later she quietly
succumbed to the blackness and slipped sideways
on to the deck.

When Alan saw Ebony, unconscious on the deck,
he nearly died. When he saw the blood, he cried
out in horror and raced forward, dropping to his
knees beside her.

'Ebony...darling,' he groaned, and shakily
picked her foot up to see what had happened.

His relief once he saw that the cut on her foot was only superficial was enormous. If anything terrible had happened to her he'd never have forgiven himself. God, whatever had possessed him to speak to her like that? It was no wonder she'd cut and run. She'd always been proud, his Ebony. Why couldn't he have made all the right noises as he'd planned, damn it? Now he'd blown everything!

A whimpering sound fluttered from her bluish lips when he scooped her up into his arms. An unconscious Ebony was affecting him even more dramatically than a weeping one. Her total helplessness brought out his male protective instinct and he cradled her against him, giving her his warmth, loving her in a way he'd never loved her before.

His Ebony...

Something strong and fiercely possessive curled around his heart as he stared down into the innocence of her unconscious face. Strangely, he knew that, no matter what she'd done with Stevenson at the Ramada, she still loved *him*. Last night did not lessen that fact. That had been just sex.

What she craved from *him* was love. Alan could see that now. That was why she'd reacted so violently to his loveless lovemaking, why it had repelled her in the end. She wanted from him what no man had ever given her before. True love.

Alan struggled to contain his emotion at this thought, but he'd been right in his resolve back at the house. He would marry her and, by God, he'd make it work. She needed him as much as he needed her. He'd watch over her, protect her, keep her safe from other men's dark desires. And her own. Everyone had faults and weaknesses. Hers was clearly sex.

But he had a plan to combat that. He'd give her a baby. Alan reasoned that maturity and the strong maternal instinct he was sure Ebony possessed would probably solve this one flaw of hers. He sure as hell hoped so, because he didn't think he could bear it if she ever made him feel again as she'd made him feel last night. Just thinking about it made him cringe. Still, that was the past, and Stevenson was going back to Paris next week. As damned hard as it would be, he would learn to forget his pain, learn to forgive.

But could he get her to forgive him?

Ah, yes...that would take some doing, if he knew his Ebony.

When she came to, it was to find herself being carried down the gangway in Alan's arms. He was wearing shorts, and nothing else, his manner grimly silent as he manoeuvred his way carefully down the steep steps and through the galley and small sitting-room. Even after several seconds she still felt totally disorientated.

'What...what happened?' she asked when he stopped at the door of the one and only bedroom.

His eyes snapped down to hers. God, but he looked dreadful, she thought dazedly, his face all pinched and strained.

'You fainted,' came his curt announcement.

'Fainted?'

'Yes, fainted. It was probably the blood.'

'The blood?' Her voice sounded weak and shaky. Slowly, she remembered something about a cut on her foot, but when she went to look at it again Alan snapped, 'Don't look! Close your eyes and try to relax.'

'All . . . all right,' she agreed, and, linking floppy arms around his bare chest, she closed her eyes and sagged back against him.

It was then that the whole scenario flooded back and she froze. What am I doing, hugging this man who doesn't love me, who only wants me for one thing?

If he noticed her sudden stiffening he ignored it, or maybe he was too busy opening the door of the cabin and getting her inside and on to the double bed.

'You'd better take that wet costume off,' he told her brusquely. 'You're frozen stiff. I'll get the first-aid kit. Here's a couple of towels.' He pulled them from the railing of the tiny *en suite* and tossed them over to her before turning and leaving.

Ebony stared at his retreating back. Frozen stiff, was she? Well, it wasn't from cold. It was from shock and horror and total despair.

A deep series of shudders rippled through her, and she realised she *was* cold. An angry desolation invaded her heart as she stripped the skimpy costume from her still damp body and threw the hateful thing into a corner. Wrapping her long wet hair up in one towel, she rubbed her shivering body with the other, then dragged the sides of the quilt around her, careful to keep her foot hanging over the edge so that any drips of blood wouldn't stain the bedspread. The floor didn't matter so much, being polished wood.

Not that she should care about his damned bedspread or his damned anything, she thought despairingly. The man was cruel and callous and so arrogantly selfish that it was mind-boggling. Did he honestly think she would marry him now? She wanted to be his wife for real, not his legal mistress, which was the only sort of marriage he seemed to have in mind, if he had one in mind at all!

Outrage welled up within her as she awaited Alan's return, yet when he walked in looking grim, then sat down to pick her foot up and stroke it with incredible softness, the angry words she'd been rehearsing couldn't seem to find voice.

'I nearly died when I found you lying unconscious on that deck,' he admitted bleakly, 'then when I saw the blood. But at least it doesn't look too deep. Still, it needs looking after...'

A lump formed in her throat while she watched him gently tend the cut, first stopping the bleeding with pressure, then disinfecting it and covering it with a large patch plaster.

'All done,' he said at last, though he continued to hold her foot, continued to touch it and stroke it in ways he knew stimulated rather than relaxed her.

The soles of her feet had always been highly sensitive in an erotic way, something which Alan had discovered and often used to his advantage. He was doing so now, narrowed blue eyes watching her reactions carefully, showing satisfaction each time she quivered. But the *coup de grâce* came when he lifted her foot to his mouth, kissing and sucking each toe in succession, his heavy-lidded eyes holding hers as he did so. By the time he finally lowered her foot back down on to the bed, she was wide-eyed and breathless.

'I'm sorry,' he murmured, continuing to stroke her feet and ankles with seductive softness. 'I shouldn't have said the things I said earlier. I know how awful they must have sounded. I don't know what possessed me. This past week has been a big strain and I was beside myself with wanting you. Say you'll forgive me, my darling. Say you still love me . . .'

Ebony blinked and swallowed. Alan had never called her his darling before. Yet some instinctive intuition at the back of her mind was whispering to her that this was a very sudden about-face and too good to be true. But to deny what he was saying was to throw away everything she'd ever dreamt about and hoped for. It was much easier to lie back and accept both Alan's assurances and caresses. Much, much easier.

She sighed when his hands began moving further up her legs, parting the quilt as he did so. His endearments were as intoxicating as his touch.

'Let me make it up to you, my darling,' he murmured thickly. 'Let me love you properly . . .'

Now he'd reached the area between her thighs and she moaned. Her mind hazed over and her legs parted on a sigh of bliss.

'God, but you're incredible,' he groaned. 'Any man would do anything to keep you ... Anything at all ...'

And he bent his mouth to her flesh.

Ebony sighed again. This was what she'd wanted; this was making love. His lips were a delight and a torment, but a very addictive torment. When he eventually moved further up her body to lick sweetly at her nipples, she felt as if she were drowning in sensations hitherto unknown to her. Her love swelled in her breast till it wasn't enough to lie there and let him make love to her. She wanted to make love back, to show him all that he meant to her.

She reached to run trembling hands over his back, lifting her head to kiss his shoulders and neck, to nibble his earlobe and run her tongue-tip around his ear. 'Take off your shorts,' she whispered shakily.

When he was naked, she reached for him, pulling him down beside her, making *him* lie still while she started kissing and touching him all over. Oh, but it was heaven to feel him tremble beneath her hands, to hear his sharply indrawn breath each time her lips moved tantalisingly close to his desire. She knew he ached to have her draw him deep into her mouth, but there was excitement in making him wait, in seeing how far she could extend his need.

She pushed him as far as she could, running her tongue-tip down the sides, then over his thighs and loins till he was quivering with expectation and tension. Only when he gave a raw, tortured groan of pain did she finally do what he so desperately wanted.

'Oh, God,' he moaned as the heat of her mouth engulfed him.

Alan stared down at the stunningly erotic picture of a naked Ebony pleasuring him that way and shuddered in sheer ecstasy. He'd had other women do this to him and had always found it arousing. But nothing could compare with the physical and emotional satisfaction he gained from having Ebony do it. Surely she must love him to make love to him so uninhibitedly. Surely she reserved this intimacy for him and him alone.

Doubts besieged him and he reached down to touch her, only to knock the towel from her head when her eyes snapped upwards. Her hair spilled around her face and she smiled at him through the damp strands. 'You want me to stop?' she teased.

'God, no...'

Now he stroked her head, telling her how much he loved her, his hips lifting and falling in a ragged rhythm of delight as she brought him closer and closer to the edge. She would have selflessly taken him all the way, he knew, but that was not either his plan or his wish. When he could bear it no more, he stopped her, pulling her up and under him so that he could sink deep inside her.

It was impossible to last long, but she didn't need long, her own aroused flesh spasming around him with a fierceness he'd never felt before. He gasped aloud, then climaxed as well, spilling himself into her for what seemed like ages. Afterwards he clasped her to him, knowing that he had never experienced the like before, and equally knowing he would never be able to give this woman up, no matter what.

Ebony sighed deeply and fell asleep in his arms, physically and emotionally sated, her confidence in Alan's love restored. When she eventually woke again, she was alone, and for a split second she felt bereft.

Sitting up, she pushed her hair out of her eyes, but she could not push the niggling feeling of disquiet out of her heart. There was no reason to feel afraid, no reason to feel anything but happy. Alan loved her. They were going to be married soon. Then they would have babies and...

Her gasp of shock sent Alan's face popping round the door. He was smiling.

'So you're awake! Why don't you have a shower, pop a towel around yourself, and come and have some lunch? Watch that foot, though. Hop, if you have to.'

'Alan!' she called after him when he disappeared.

He reappeared in the doorway, all of him this time. He was now wearing his shirt as well as shorts. 'Yes?'

'I just realised. You... you didn't use anything. When we made love...'

His shrug was dismissive. 'I forgot to bring them with me. Does it really matter? We'll be married soon. Besides, you'd have to be unlucky to get pregnant straight away.'

'I...I don't know about that. It's a dangerous time for me...'

Alan came forward and sat down on the side of the bed, taking her hands in his. His eyes were intent as they raked hers. 'I thought you said you wanted children.'

'I do! But I...I——'

'You what?' he said sharply.

Ebony stared into Alan's suddenly cold blue eyes and felt a resurgence of that earlier unease. It wasn't like Alan to forget anything. It wasn't like him at all.

But how could she accuse the man she loved of trying to trap her into a pregnancy? Why would he feel he had to trap her anyway? She did want children, but she'd hoped having a baby would be something they would plan together, a mutual decision made with thought and love. Still, it seemed silly to quibble at this stage. What was done was done.

'Oh, nothing.' She tried a smile, but it felt somewhat forced. 'I guess we'll just have to wait and see, won't we? I might have to buy a specially designed wedding-dress that hides tummies.'

'I doubt that. We'll be getting married within a couple of months.'

'So soon?' she gasped.

'Why should we wait? I'm not getting any younger and I've waited long enough for you, surely?'

'I . . . I guess so.'

He cupped her face and kissed her. 'I'll take you somewhere deliciously private for our honeymoon.'

'Such as?'

'How about a dungeon?' he said with a dark chuckle.

Though startled, she laughed. 'What are you? The Marquis de Sade reincarnated?'

'Could be, Ebony. Could be.'

She smiled a loving amusement at that thought. 'Not you, Alan. You like to play the big, bad wolf, but underneath you're a sweet, cuddly bear.'

'Even bears can be dangerous, my darling.' He smiled back, and bent to kiss her once more. 'Always remember that,' he whispered, and patted her gently on the cheek. 'Now get up, woman. Bob's picnic lunch awaits.'

CHAPTER ELEVEN

'This is the life,' Alan sighed, leaning back against the booth-style seat and lifting the glass of wine to his lips. They'd already finished one bottle of Chardonnay between them and had moved on to the second. Bob's picnic lunch of crispy fried chicken plus his special pasta salad and herb bread had long been reduced to crumbs and bones.

Ebony was sitting opposite, wrapped in a towel, her face washed clean of make-up. She looked about sixteen, Alan conceded, his gut tightening at the thought that she'd probably already been pleasuring men's bodies back at sixteen, or even younger.

For a second he felt fiercely, insanely jealous, but then he took a sharp hold of himself. I'll have to control my jealousy if I'm going to marry her, he vowed. Either that or I'll go stark raving mad.

There again, it's only normal for a husband to want to know all there is to know about his wife. What do I know about Ebony before she came to live with Mother and myself? It's not as though Pierre and Judith lived just around the corner. I was lucky to see them once a year.

Alan stared down into the near empty glass as he twirled it slowly in his hands. A degree of puzzlement filtered in when he realised he'd avoided

151

the subject of Ebony's childhood for years. Why?
What was he afraid of finding out?

He looked up, blue eyes hardening as he determined to ask about her life with her parents.

'Yes?' She cocked her head on one side and
smiled at him. There was a quality of innocence
about that smile that curled around his heart. Damn
it all, he didn't want to find out anything that would
destroy that illusion of innocence. Not now. Not
today.

'Yes what?' he asked with deliberate vagueness.

Her smile became knowing. 'You were going to
ask me a question. I saw it in your eyes.'

His own smile felt forced. 'I'm glad you're not
a business adversary, reading my face like that. I
was simply wondering how your foot was. Is it
hurting you?'

'It throbs a little.'

'Do you want some pain-killers?'

'No. Just pour me some more of this wine. It's
delicious.'

'It is rather good.' He filled her glass to the brim
then emptied the rest into his own. 'That's the last
of it, I'm afraid, though I do have some other wine
around here somewhere. Not Chardonnay, though,
and not chilled. Shall I put a bottle in the re-
frigerator for later?'

'By all means. Might as well take advantage of
the fact that you don't have to drive home.'

'Speaking of home,' Alan found himself saying
while he rummaged around in the galley cupboards
in search of the wine, 'it must have been hard on

you not having a proper home while growing up. I mean . . . you mostly lived in rented apartments and hotel rooms, didn't you?'

And so much for his decision to let sleeping dogs lie . . .

Ebony's silence drew him to glance over his shoulder at her. 'Aren't you going to answer me?'

No way could he read *her* face. Ebony was a mistress of deception when she wanted to be. But while those coal-black eyes of hers had glazed into an expressionless void, her body language bespoke a tension that was unmistakable. She didn't want to talk about her childhood. Even having been *reminded* of it was upsetting her.

'Ebony?'

'Really, Alan, haven't we got more interesting things to talk about besides my boring old childhood?'

A surge of something close to panic claimed him. What in hell lay buried in her past that was so ghastly that she had to put on this pretence of cool indifference?

Several ideas infiltrated, all of them horrifying. Dear God, surely she hadn't been sexually abused, had she? He'd read about such victims often becoming promiscuous as a result of either being raped or abused as a child. It seemed too vile to contemplate, although such a tragic background might explain the mystery of Ebony's behaviour with other men.

Alan paled, but kept his face turned away till he found the wine. If she had been abused in some way, she wasn't likely to blurt it out. She would have to be coaxed into telling the truth. Extracting two bottles of white burgundy from the back of the cupboard, he turned to put them in the small gas fridge before sitting back down opposite her.

'It seems only reasonable that I want to know all about you,' he said smoothly. 'I love you, Ebony. Very much.'

His assertion of love discomfited her, or was it his persistence in asking about the past?

'You already know everything there is to know, surely?' she said with a dismissive shrug.

She was hedging, he could tell, her eyes evading his by pretending to look down at the plaster on her foot.

'Not really,' he replied. 'Because of Pierre's and Judith's constant travelling, I didn't get to spend much time with them. Or you. If your parents hadn't had the misfortune to be on that ferry that day when it capsized, I would never have got to know you at all.'

Her eyes jerked to his, smouldering with an intensity that startled him. 'But you did. And you know what? My parents' misfortune was my good fortune. Because it meant coming to live with you and your mother. God, even the boarding-school you sent me to was preferable to living with them.' Her involuntary shudder of revulsion shocked Alan. 'I hated living with them. Maybe I even hated *them*,' she bit out.

Alan stared at her. My God, was the situation worse than he'd been envisaging? Had the abuse come from within the family? But who? What?

'That's a very strong thing to say about your parents, Ebony.' He managed to sound calmer than he felt. 'From what I could see, they loved you very much.'

Now those black eyes blazed with indignation. 'Did they?' She shook her head. 'Well, maybe Papa did in his own selfish way, especially since I looked like him. But not Mama. She never loved me. She only had me because she thought a child would bind Papa to her forever. She never had any love left over for me.'

Alan almost sighed with relief. This was not as bad as he'd been fearing. Daughters often thought mothers didn't love them, especially when competing for their father's love. He'd heard the same complaints from Vicki when she'd been about thirteen. Still, he had to agree with Ebony that her parents had seemed rather self-absorbed in their lifestyle.

'I'm sure Judith loved you,' he soothed. 'She was a very warm woman.'

'How would you know what Mama was?' Ebony challenged. 'By your own admission you hardly ever saw my parents.'

'Maybe not after they got married, but I knew your mother quite well beforehand.'

'You did?'

'Judith was my father's secretary for years. Didn't you know?'

Ebony was clearly astonished by this news.

So was Alan by her reaction. 'Didn't your mother ever tell you how she met your father?' he asked incredulously.

'Never. She—er—didn't really talk to me about anything much. Neither did Papa for that matter.'

Alan frowned. It sounded as if Ebony's parents had been more than selfish in their treatment of their daughter. Downright neglectful seemed closer to the mark. He recalled his own mother having commented about Ebony's 'withdrawn' manner shortly after coming to live with them. At the time, he'd thought it grief. Now he saw it for what it was: intense loneliness.

God, he must have been blind back then not to notice how grateful Ebony had been for any crumbs of affection and attention. She'd fairly glowed when he and his mother had made the effort to show up for every single one of her school functions, and then whenever he'd taken her out in the holidays. Hell, the child had been literally *starved* for love. He could see that now.

Yet it seemed *Judith* had been the guiltier party when it had come to withholding affection, a fact which surprised him. As he'd told Ebony, she'd always seemed a sensitive woman, not like Pierre, who'd never struck Alan as a man of any great emotional depth. Admittedly, he was charming and intelligent, and his generous loan of money after Alan's father's death had been a godsend. It had come out later, however, that Pierre had been a risk-taker of the first order. He'd made many wild investments. Some had paid off. Others hadn't. In the end, most hadn't, and he'd died stony broke.

'Well, as I said,' Alan went on when he realised Ebony was waiting for him to continue, 'Judith was my father's secretary. That's how she first came to meet Pierre. He was in Australia buying wool for a large French manufacturing company and he visited Dad's clothing factory to see some of the fine woollen garments made here. Dad brought him home for dinner a couple of times. I was only a boy at the time and found him quite fascinating.'

'Papa could be very fascinating,' Ebony agreed drily. 'When he needed to be.'

'What do you mean by that exactly?'

'I mean when he wanted to impress a woman. I presume your father brought his secretary to these dinners to make up the numbers?'

'I think she came to one.'

'And Papa took Mama home afterwards?'

'I can't really recall.'

Ebony smiled a smile that chilled Alan's bones. 'He would have. And he would have stayed the night. What has always puzzled me is why he married Mama at all. It wasn't to have children. He didn't like them particularly, though I think he was almost fond of me.'

'More than fond, I would think. But maybe your mother was not as accommodating as you have presumed, Ebony. Maybe she was not that kind of girl.'

'Or maybe she was simply cleverer than the others. You know what, Alan? I think you're right.

I think she refused to sleep with him. That's the only thing that would have got Papa to the altar, of that I'm sure.'

'There is another solution,' he suggested, finding her cynicism unnerving. 'Pierre might have truly fallen in love with Judith.'

'Papa?' Ebony laughed. 'Don't be ridiculous, Alan. He had no concept of true love.'

'He never divorced her.'

'Which wasn't because he loved her, though she did love him, if one could call what she felt—love. I call it a sickness. There was nothing she wouldn't do for him, including turning a blind eye to his bedding every available woman he could get his hands on. Of course, when it was someone under her own roof, she did fire them. Over the years, I lost count of the number of nannies and companions and tutors and housekeepers we had. It wasn't till I caught Papa with one of them in bed that I realised what was going on.'

'God, Ebony,' Alan groaned. 'What a rotten atmosphere for a young girl to grow up in.'

'To be honest, it wasn't the sexual goings-on that upset me as much as not ever being able to form a close relationship with anyone. I dared not bring girlfriends home and I learnt not to make friends with the women Mama employed, because I knew they wouldn't last. People used to think I was weird. I wasn't. I simply chose to distance myself from those around me because it was less hurtful not to care about anyone in the first place.'

Alan felt dismay and sadness that Ebony's life had been so wretched. 'Wasn't there anyone you could confide in, or feel close to? An aunt or uncle, perhaps?'

'We never visited relatives. As for my parents' friends...they weren't the type of people one could confide in. Why do you think Papa made you my guardian in his will? You were the only person he'd ever had dealings with of any honour, or principle.'

Guilt curled within Alan's stomach. Some principle he'd proved to have. Still, at least he was prepared to marry the girl, despite her appalling upbringing. But no wonder she wasn't normal, sexually. She herself admitted that she hadn't been upset by her father's excesses in the end. Her sense of right and wrong had probably been dulled by constant exposure to immoral behaviour.

'Don't look so serious, Alan. You have to admit living with Mama and Papa gave me a broad mind in certain matters.'

'Judith should have at least put you in boarding-school,' Alan muttered. 'You shouldn't have had to put up with—or witness—the things you did. Your father's behaviour was a very bad example for a growing girl's mind.'

Ebony shrugged and picked up her wine glass to drink, her nonchalance provoking him.

'Can't you see it made you think promiscuity was normal?' he accused.

Her black eyes flashed then narrowed as they met his over the rim of the glass, but she said nothing till she had taken a swallow of the wine.

'You've always believed I was promiscuous, haven't you?' she said bitterly. 'When exactly do you believe I started having sex? How old?'

Now it was his turn to shrug, but it was an uncomfortable gesture, not an indifferent one.

'Eighteen?' she suggested.

What did she see in his face to make her look at him like that?

'Sixteen?' she tried, half disbelievingly.

When he declined to answer, she stared at him.

'My God, how low could I go before I get some sign of agreement?' she went on savagely. 'Fourteen, perhaps? Twelve, even? Answer me, damn you!'

'I'm waiting for you to tell me,' he replied, agitated by her self-righteous anger. Why couldn't she just admit she'd started young? He wouldn't condemn her for it. He could see now she hadn't had much of a chance to be different. Pierre had set the pattern in the household and she had absorbed his morals without even being aware of it.

'If I recall rightly, I told you all this once before, Alan,' she bit out. 'There's only been one man before you, and I was twenty at the time.'

His sigh was full of scepticism and exasperation. Had she honestly expected him to believe that? Even if it *was* true, by some miracle, it didn't alter her present promiscuity. She'd spent most of last night with that bastard photographer, then come away on this boat with him this morning without a qualm.

The memory of Stevenson kissing her good-night, of her laughter afterwards, speared Alan with a sudden and savage jealousy. It took all his mental strength to gather himself and not confront her then and there with his knowledge.

'So you did,' he replied coldly. 'And was Stevenson a good lover?'

'Was Adrianna?' she countered, not so coldly.

Steely blue eyes snapped to blazing black ones. 'I don't think that's on a par, do you?'

'No, I don't. I didn't love Gary, which makes him far less of a rival for my affections than Adrianna is for yours. You loved her, or so you always claimed. Where does she figure in your life these days, Alan? Is our marriage bed to have a ghost in it, or can I be assured your love is all mine?'

Alan glared frustration at Ebony. Damn it, but the witch was turning things around, twisting the facts. Why should he be made to feel any guilt about his relationship with Adrianna? They might not have been in love, but they had been good to each other. There'd been no mad jealousies or hurting involved, and when it had finished it had finished cleanly.

'Were you in love with her or not?' Ebony persisted in asking. 'I think I have a right to know.'

'Why? What gives you the right to know anything about my life before I became involved with you? Why can't the past be the past?'

'Because it isn't. The past can taint the future. Is my past past for you? If so, why were you quizzing me about it just now? What would it matter if I'd screwed every man I met before you as long as I stopped after I did?'

'But you didn't, did you?' he lashed out without being able to stop himself. 'You used to taunt me with all your other lovers all the time, remember?'

Her face flushed a bright red, but she kept her chin up, her eyes proud and strong. 'I lied. I wanted to make you jealous. And why not? You gave me nothing, Alan, except your body in bed. Not a kind word or a scrap of love. I needed to see your jealousy to soothe my own love, to keep clinging to the thin hope that you did care about me. He wouldn't be jealous, I used to tell myself, if he didn't love me a little.'

Alan jumped up, shaking inside with emotion. 'And were you trying to make me jealous last night when you went to Stevenson's hotel room, when you made love to him for hours on end, when you let him kiss you goodnight in front of everyone, including me?'

Ebony's mouth dropped open, her shock overwhelming. And then she crumpled.

'Oh, God,' she groaned, her head dropping into her hands. 'God . . .'

'No speech in defence?' he jeered. 'No claim of total innocence or mistaken identity?'

She shook her head, muttering something he couldn't hear.

Well, he'd blown it now, all right. And he didn't care. Goddamn it, what man could have been that noble to forgive and forget such treachery? He certainly wasn't. His crazy idea of marrying her and saving her from herself had been just that. Crazy! Worry over her faithless nature would eventually have torn his guts out.

Just looking at her bowed head—her obvious *guilt*—was sending a raging fury along his veins, making his blood boil and his head pound.

'Look at me, you two-timing bitch!' he spat.

Her head jerked up, her eyes blurred with tears.

'Oh, no,' he mocked with a harsh bark of laughter. 'That won't work this time, honey. I've been there, done that. This time I want to hear word for word what you did with that bastard. I want to hear you explain how you can sleep with him last night and claim you love me today. I've tried to understand it. Maybe I even do, but I can't live with it. I thought I could. I even thought if we had a baby together, then we might have been able to make a go of it, that you would settle down and stop craving sexual excitement. But that wouldn't have stopped you, would it? There would always be a Stevenson in one form or another. You're just like your father, aren't you?

'*Aren't you*?' he screamed at her, thumping the table with a balled fist.

He watched her rise, watched her blink away the tears, watched her gather that steely inner strength that he'd always admired, however reluctantly.

'No,' she denied vehemently. 'I'm not like my father. Not in the least. Not that I expect you to believe me. As for what I did last night with Gary, I'll tell you. I had dinner with him in his hotel room because he's my friend and he's going away. I didn't go to a restaurant because I was afraid someone might see us together and jump to the wrong conclusions, something that has plagued me for years. We ate, we talked—about you, actually,' she added with a sardonic laugh. 'Ironic, isn't it?'

She laughed again, then slumped back down in the seat, her shoulders and head drooping. She felt utterly devastated and totally defeated. Who would have believed Alan would see her and Gary together? What twist of fate would have brought him to the Ramada at that time of night and at that precise moment? God, but life could be cruel . . .

'Do go on,' Alan snapped. 'Don't stop now. I can see you're as good at lying as you are in bed.'

Ebony looked up at him with desolation in her eyes.

'I have very little else to say. There are some people who don't wish to believe, no matter what the evidence or explanations may be. You're one of those people, Alan. Oh, I appreciate I have played a role in the opinion you've formed of me, but only a very small role. You've always been happy to believe the worst. I could slap a private-detective report in front of you, proving that I was as pure as the driven snow when I wasn't with you, and you wouldn't believe it. Yet it is the truth, Alan. I've never touched another man in a sexual sense since we became lovers.'

'What about the kiss I saw Stevenson give you?' came the harsh accusation. 'That wasn't my imagination.'

'Neither was it anything for you to worry about,' she replied wearily. 'A goodbye kiss, for pity's sake. The man's been very good to me.'

'But by your own admission, he'd once been your lover,' Alan argued. 'He also asked you to marry him quite recently. And you were going to for a while. Goddamn it, Ebony, I have every reason to be suspicious and jealous. Don't take me for a fool!' And he banged the table with a balled fist, the intimidating and violent action firing an answering fury within her.

'And don't take me for a tramp!' she flung back fiercely, tossing her hair back from her bared shoulders and glaring up at him. 'I'm not. I was a virgin when I went to bed with Gary. I only let him seduce me because I was so lonely and I thought I would never have you. God, I cried and cried afterwards because I'd only ever wanted you, and anything else was second-best. I never loved Gary and I was never going to marry him. I only said that as a desperate escape because I couldn't go on being your mistress. It was killing me, Alan. Really killing me.' Tears flooded her eyes again and this time Alan could not remain unmoved.

Dear God, but all she'd just said had the ring of truth about it. And it stabbed his heart with pain and regret. What if she wasn't lying? He dropped back down on to the seat, the air rushing from his lungs.

'I'm not like my father,' she sobbed quietly. 'All I ever wanted was for you to love me as I loved you. Oh, I know you think I couldn't have fallen in love with you at fifteen. But I did. I know I did. You meant the world to me, right from the first day you brought me into your home. You were everything my father wasn't. You were hard-working and honest and kind. Your family was everything my family wasn't as well, with your loving concern for each other, your warmth and your generosity.'

'You...you didn't seem to like my generosity,' he muttered unhappily, and, picking up a paper serviette, reached over and pressed it into her hand. 'Blow your nose. It's dripping.'

Her smile was softly wry as she did as he told her.

'Most people might conclude I was merely a father-figure to you, Ebony,' he pronounced firmly, trying to keep his head when all he really wanted to do was sweep her up into his arms, to hold her and kiss her and make beautiful love to her. He didn't want to talk about the past any more. He wanted to forget all their misunderstandings and just go forward. But perhaps this was necessary, this purging. He doubted their relationship could survive any more secret revelations.

She was nodding in quiet agreement. 'And they'd probably be right. To begin with. But you soon became much more, Alan. I didn't want you as my father for long. I wanted you as my lover.

'Oh, yes,' she swept on, seeing his knee-jerk re-action to her statement. 'It's true and I'm not ashamed of it. By the time I was seventeen I was wanting you in my bed. I lay awake many a night thinking about it, fantasising about all the things we could do together. Maybe in that I am like my father. I don't think of sex itself as shameful, only how people abuse and misuse it. Sex is a very powerful and natural drive, and, while people seem to accept that young men have it on their minds all the time, so do young women, believe me. I wasn't at all unusual. Most of my girlfriends at school were just as fascinated by the subject.'

'Maybe so, Ebony, but sex is not love. I can understand that I might have been the object of your youthful romantic fantasies. What other man did you have in your life, after all? No one. But you weren't in love with me. Not back then.'

Her laughter surprised him. 'Dear Alan, how naïve you are sometimes for a grown man. Don't you think I met boys down the street, or at the beach or the school discos I went to? I had plenty of opportunity for experimentation, if that was all I wanted. Then after I left your home to live by myself in a flat I had oodles of very attractive men throwing themselves at me, doing everything they could think of to get me into their beds. They didn't succeed because I didn't love them.'

'Stevenson succeeded.'

Ebony closed her eyes. 'Yes . . .'

'Why was he different?' Alan asked bleakly. 'You said you didn't love him.'

She sighed and opened her eyes. They were still blurred, he saw, and his heart turned over.

'I liked him.' She shrugged. 'We'd been working together for a long time. And he caught me at a vulnerable moment.'

'Vulnerable in what way?'

'I...I'd been over to the house to visit your mother the day before. I don't know if you recall the occasion, but you...you looked up at me when I came in—you were having lunch at the time—and you didn't say a single word. You just put down your serviette, stood up and left. I know why you acted that way now, but I didn't then, and it...it was my birthday, Alan,' she choked out. 'My twentieth birthday...'

His groan was full of pain. 'Your birthdays have really been disaster days where I'm concerned, haven't they? God, Ebony, I'm sorry...for everything. I've really made a mess of things, haven't I?'

'No more than I. We have to learn to forgive ourselves, Alan, and appreciate the favour fate did us by throwing us together. I know you still think you're too old for me, but you're not. You're perfect for me.'

His smile was wry. 'You have a penchant for older men?'

'I think I do,' she replied quite seriously. 'After watching my father's womanising for years, I needed a strong, stable man who would make me feel totally secure in his love. Could a man of my own age do that? I doubt it. And you know what? I think one of the reasons you fell in love with me was *my* age. I think you responded to my youth because it revived in you what circumstances forced you to miss—*your* youth, with all its lust and passion. I brought you alive, Alan, as no older woman could bring you alive.

'Even Adrianna,' she finished with a tight squeezing of her chest. Lord, would she never get rid of her jealousy over that woman? Would it always hurt that he had loved her first, loved her better? Oh, it wasn't the sex part. She could cope with that. It was Alan's heart she coveted, his soul. She needed to feel he was *all* hers, not just his body. She'd meant it when she'd said she didn't want a ghost in bed with them.

'Adrianna,' he repeated with a dark frown, and Ebony felt a stab of something akin to real panic. What was he thinking about to make him look so worried, so...guilty?

Ebony didn't feel she could let the moment go. She had to know. *Had* to!

'What is it?' she asked quite sharply. 'What haven't you told me about you and Adrianna?'

His glance was more than worried now. 'I have something I must tell you which I hope you'll understand.'

'What?' she managed to ask in a strangled tone.

'Last night, I—er—well, the truth is that—um...'

Ebony didn't need him to say it. The truth—for want of a better word—jumped into her brain with crystal-clear clarity. The businessman Alan had had dinner with had not been a man at all. The ghost who walked had walked back into their lives.

'You had dinner with Adrianna,' she said flatly. 'It wasn't a business dinner at all...'

His face told so much. 'Don't jump to conclusions, for God's sake.'

Don't jump to conclusions? What kind of conclusions? That he'd slept with her? It was hard to think he'd slept with her in a restaurant. Unless...

Various pieces of the puzzle of last night began to slide into place. Ebony's eyes widened with horror and understanding. 'She was staying at the Ramada, wasn't she?' she accused. 'You brought her back to the hotel after dinner, didn't you? That's how you came to be there to see me with Gary.'

'Ebony, don't do this. Remember the false conclusions I jumped to with Gary. You'll be just as wrong if you start thinking anything happened between Adrianna and me last night. She's a happily married woman. She's six months pregnant. I did not sleep with her or do anything wrong. I gave her a goodnight peck on the cheek, that's all.'

Emotion impelled Ebony on to her feet, her black eyes blazing down at him. 'I don't believe you!' she flung at him heatedly. 'You kissed her, you bastard. You went through the roof about Gary and me, when all the time you'd been in that woman's arms yourself. You *do* still love her. You'll always love her. Stop denying it!'

The pain behind her accusation became a scream in her head and she couldn't bear it any more. Scrambling out from behind the table, she fled for the gangway in a blind rush, unsure of where she

was going or what she was about to do. Her reaction when Alan grabbed her ankle from behind
before she could reach the top of the narrow
staircase was both violent and wild. Swinging
round, she kicked out at him, but he side-stepped
and somehow scooped her unbalanced self up off
the steps and into his steely arms.

'And where did you think you were going?' he
demanded harshly. 'Into the river again? There'll
be no more blind running away, Ebony. And no
more misunderstandings between us. We're going
to talk this out, and, by God, you're going to really
listen to me this time!'

And so saying, he carried her down the narrow
walkway into the one place where talking was the
last thing they'd ever done. The bedroom.

CHAPTER TWELVE

ALAN kicked the door shut behind him, more from lack of room than temper. Ebony was an armful. Angling himself down the side of the built-in bed, he would have lowered her gently on to the quilt if she hadn't chosen that moment to struggle.

'Let me go, you brute. I've had enough of your manhandling tactics, not to mention your hypocritical and typically male double standards!'

He dumped her on the bed. A silly thing to do. The towel that had already been slipping precariously down over her breasts burst asunder. Alan groaned silently and tried to put his mind on the problem at hand.

Which was what? Damn, but he could hardly remember.

'Cover yourself up,' he growled, and spun away to drag in a steadying breath before turning to face Ebony once more.

She lay there, the towel now draped across the middle of her body as if she were awaiting a massage, her chin tipped defiantly up at him. But her eyes . . . Dear God, her eyes revealed a despair he hated seeing.

I've done this to her, he agonised. I've mis-judged her, tormented her, crucified her. I've taken her love, taken her body, taken her pride.

No, he amended. Never her pride. Never that . . .

'I'm waiting, Alan,' she snapped, her pride and spirit very much intact. 'Make it good, though.'

He frowned. 'Good?'

'The reason why I should believe there was nothing between you and Adrianna on Friday night, whereas *I* was condemned as a whore over my date with Gary. After all, you loved Adrianna once enough to ask her to marry you. Whereas *I* . . . I turned down Gary's offer of marriage because I'd never loved him!'

He groaned and grimaced at the same time. Hoist with his own petard! He should never have given in to the temptation to keep fuelling Ebony's jealousy with his supposed love of Adrianna. It had been cruel and so unnecessary. He bitterly regretted it now, because it made convincing her of the truth all the more difficult. Yet he had to try, didn't he?

Alan came forward, Ebony flinching with fear when he sat down beside her on the bed. He'd always used sex to get his own way with her. And she'd always surrendered in the end. But dear God, not this time, *please* . . .

Everything inside her tightened when he picked up her hand. But he simply held it within both of his and started speaking in a low, measured tone.

'I realise this probably comes too late. But they say "better late than never" . . .'

Ebony was astonished to see his mouth soften into a rueful yet touching smile. 'I did ask Adrianna to marry me, I admit. But it wasn't because I loved her. We were good friends and we drifted into an affair, but we were never in love. Neither of us. Just two lonely people reaching out to each other as you reached out to Stevenson.'

Ebony blinked her astonishment. 'But...but *why* did you ask her to marry you, if you didn't love her?'

'Why, indeed? Can't you think of a reason, my darling?'

She shook her head, her fluttering heart still not used to Alan calling her his darling. And to think he'd never loved Adrianna. But dared she believe him? What was this mysterious reason?

'I asked Adrianna to marry me to protect the sweet innocence of a girl I believed was too young for love, a girl who twisted my heart and body into knots every time I saw her.'

Ebony stared, her heart leaping. So she'd been right all along. He *had* wanted her back then.

'Yes, it was you I really wanted, Ebony, not Adrianna, you I loved, even though I could not accept that at the time. Maybe if you'd been anyone else other than my ward, I might have seen what a surprisingly mature young woman you were, and that you were as capable of giving true love as receiving it. As it was, I was consumed by guilt at desiring an innocent who'd been entrusted to my care. So I set about saving you from my carnal lust, protecting you from my dark desires...'

His low laugh carried a wealth of remembered pain. 'I imagined a wife would be the perfect antidote for my forbidden feelings. But the best-laid plans of mere mortal men come unstuck sometimes. When Adrianna married Bryce McLean instead, I had to resort to whatever tactics would keep you safe. I was rude and cruel and hurtful. Every time you came within a hundred feet of me I deliberately drove you away. I was almost insane with frustration, and eventually it began to come out in the worst possible way...'

He shook his head, his expression grim. Ebony carefully extracted her hand from where he'd started squeezing her fingers tightly through emotion. It brought his eyes up with a worried jerk, but she merely smiled at him and wiggled her fingers. 'They were going to sleep.'

Alan was moved by her sweetly loving smile. God, but he'd been a stupid bastard to believe all the rotten things he'd believed about her. But that was what he was trying to explain now. Would she listen? Would she understand? Would she forgive him? What if she didn't? What if...?

No, no, he couldn't think like that. She would understand, his Ebony. She would understand and forgive, because she really truly loved him. He gulped down one last lump of anguish and went on.

'I tried to hate you,' he confessed. 'I wallowed in every scrap of scandal and gossip I heard about you. I filed them away in my tormented mind, exaggerated them, hugged them to my ever increasing need to justify the feelings I hadn't been able to conquer. She's wicked, I told myself. A corruptress. A seductress. A pagan goddess. It's not my fault I want her as I do. All men want her. And she wants all men. I could have her if I really wanted her. But how could I possibly want someone so cheap and disgustingly easy? Oh, the lies I kept clinging to in order to stop myself from doing what I was dying to do.'

Ebony's eyes were wide upon him, appalled yet fascinated.

'Perhaps if I'd gone to bed with another woman. But I didn't *want* another woman! You were all I wanted all those years, yet all I did was make you miserable. My Ebony, my love, and I was *vile* to you.' He shook his head, his shoulders sagging. 'God...'

'Alan, stop,' she said gently, reaching to take his hand in hers this time. 'Let it go.'

'Let what go?'

'The guilt. We've found each other now. I love you and you love me and it's futile to torment ourselves with the past. I've done crazy things too. Look at the way I tortured *you* with my innuendoes about other men. No matter how sorry I am for that now I can't take it back. We were both wrong. We must forgive ourselves, as well as each other.

We must go on and resolve to be happy together. We deserve it.'

Her smile was like a physical blow to Alan, because it meant so much. She forgave him. She understood him. She still loved him.

And then she did something so bold and brave and beautiful that he almost cried. She swept aside that towel, held her arms out, and simply said, 'Darling...'

The next half-hour would live in Alan's mind forever as an example of the most perfect love-making. Yet there was no wild passion, no torrid mating, no Kama Sutra position or exceptionally erotic foreplay. It was as though they were making love for the first time and it was enough to just hold her and stroke her softly, his fingers trembling slightly as they traced the glorious shape of her body, revelling in the knowledge that she would always be his and his alone.

The splendour of her love kept washing through him in waves of bittersweet emotion, and eventually he had to bury his face in her breast to hide his eyes lest she think him a fool. But she would have none of that, cupping his face and lifting it to hers so that she could kiss his damp cheeks and his suddenly tremulous mouth.

'I adore, you,' she whispered, and kissed him again. 'Now give me that baby, my darling. But give it to me slowly...'

He laughed, feeling heady with desire as he eased his aching flesh into her hot velvet depths. God, but she felt incredible. *She* was incredible.

I'll make it up to her, he thought as he set up a steady but powerful rhythm. I'll give her anything she wants, anything at all. Nothing will be too much trouble.

Her gasps brought him back to the present and as he saw her eyes shut and her lips part on a soft moan of ecstasy he thought he would never hear anything so satisfying as the sounds of her pleasure. But then his own pleasure took control of his mind and he was drowning in their love, drowning in *her*, simply drowning...

Afterwards, he held her close, and promised her the world.

'If you like,' he murmured, 'I'll even buy us a new house to start our married life in. I know Mother can be a bit interfering and——'

'Oh, but we couldn't do that!' Ebony burst out, pushing away from the warmth of his broad chest to stare up at him, her face aghast. 'She'd be devastated! And so would poor Bob and Bill. Why, you're their world, Alan, don't you know that?'

'I wouldn't go that far...'

'I don't mind living with your mother. Really I don't. In fact, it would be good to have a built-in baby-sitter. We could still have weekends away together, and...and...well, quite frankly, Alan, I...I have some other plans as well. For a career.'

Now Alan was frowning at her. 'I thought you said you would happily give up modelling. Oh, my God, you're not thinking of becoming an actress, are you?'

'Heavens, no. I don't want to see another camera ever again. Or a catwalk, for that matter. What I want to do is go back to college and become an infant teacher. I realise you'd have to support me while I did that, Alan, but I'd pay you back. Really I would. Once I was working, I could——'

'Stop!' he ground out, both his hands reaching up to rub his temples.

'What's wrong? Are you ill? Are you in pain?'

'I have a feeling I'm going to be in pain for the next fifty years,' he groaned.

Ebony felt bewildered as Alan's hands dropped away to take her firmly by the shoulders. 'I don't want to hear one more word about your paying me back,' he told her sternly. 'For *anything*. I am a rich man and I love you. Let me bestow my worldly goods on you as the marriage vows say. Let me love you and cherish you as a slightly old-fashioned husband wants to love and cherish his wife.'

Ebony's heart turned over. 'That's what I want too, Alan,' she whispered. 'To be loved and cher-ished in an old-fashioned way.'

'Good. Now put your head back down here and shut up. I like cuddling with my wife-to-be.'

'I like my husband-to-be cuddling me,' she laughed softly.

With a sigh, she settled back into his arms, listening contentedly to the sound of his heart beating strongly in his chest. Her eyes closed and she felt the love pulsate between them.

'Ebony,' Alan whispered after a while.

'Mmm?'

'I don't really want you to become old-fashioned, you know. I like the woman you are. I like your rampant sexuality and your——'

'My *what* sexuality?' she broke in, clearly bewildered.

'Rampant.'

She lifted her head to look up at him, but her hair fell into her eyes. Moving to straddle him, she sat up, pushing the tangled strands back from her face and shoulders with unconsciously sensual movements. 'What does rampant mean?'

Alan's breath caught in his throat when she bent forward to kiss him lightly on the mouth, her erect nipples brushing his chest.

'Is it good or bad?' she asked with the most arousing ingenuousness.

'Good,' he rasped.

'But what does it *mean*?'

'I'll tell you afterwards,' he growled, and, splaying both his hands up into her hair, he pulled her mouth down hard on to his.

Deirdre Carstairs was stretched out on the cane lounger in the sun-room, browsing through the Sunday papers and having a late, leisurely brunch when she saw Alan and Ebony making their way, hand in hand, up the back steps and across the terrace. The sun was just setting, throwing a warm glow over their dark heads. They stopped once to kiss lightly, smiling their happiness at each other.

Deirdre's heart swelled with joy and wonderment. She could not have chosen a more perfect spouse for her son. God had been very good to her the day that he'd directed Ebony into their household. As a mother, she'd been so afraid Alan would never get married and have children, that she would never have grandchildren. But one look at those two together confirmed her suspicion that it wouldn't be long before there was the patter of little feet around these empty old rooms.

Suddenly, she noticed that Ebony was limping slightly. Rising, Deirdre hurried to meet them just as they were coming through the French doors.

'Ebony, dear, have you hurt yourself?' she asked straight away.

'Just a small cut on her foot, Mother,' Alan reassured. 'She's fine, aren't you, darling?'

Deirdre just stopped herself from staring at her son. He just wasn't the type to call anyone 'darling'. It just showed how much in love he was. 'You had a nice relaxing weekend, then?'

'*Very* relaxing,' Ebony said, and flashed Alan an incredibly sexy smile.

Deirdre beamed with satisfaction. This beautiful young thing was just what the doctor ordered for Alan. He'd been in danger of turning into somewhat of a stuffed shirt before she had burst back into his life. His claim that she'd shamelessly seduced him on the night of her twenty-first was probably a blatant exaggeration. Deirdre suspected Alan was a bit of a prude where sex was concerned. That Adrianna he'd got mixed up with had been a bit of a cold fish. Ebony was completely the opposite. There again, French girls were notorious for their sensuality.

'By the way, Mother,' Alan began, 'go right ahead and plan that engagement party. As soon as possible too. Ebony and I are getting married as quickly as the law allows.'

Now Deirdre could not hide her surprise, or her smugness. 'Is there—er—some reason for the hurry?'

'We're not sure yet, but better safe than sorry, wouldn't you say?'

'Yes, indeed. Next weekend for the party, then? I'll organise everything.' She clapped her hands excitedly. 'Oh, how exciting. I'll go tell Bob and Bill. They'll be tickled pink. Then I'll ring Vicki and . . .'

She was still bubbling away as she left the room, after which Alan turned to draw Ebony into his arms, kissing her resoundingly. She pulled back at last, laughing with soft surprise at this new and rather shameless Alan. He didn't even seem to mind who knew what they'd been up to all weekend.

'Your mother was pleased,' she said.

'Who wouldn't be, having a daughter-in-law like you?'

She flushed with pleasure at his words.

'You are so giving, my darling. Not many women would care about their mother-in-law's happiness, only someone as special and sweet as you.' His hands curved softly around her face, lifting her chin so that her lips tipped up to his. 'Of course, you do have another side to your character,' he murmured softly into her mouth. 'One which will remain for my eyes only...'

When the telephone ringing interrupted their kiss, Alan glared at it for a second before disentangling himself from Ebony's arms and resignedly snatching up the receiver. 'Alan Carstairs,' he announced a touch brusquely.

'Alan, it's Vicki.'

'Vicki! I'm glad you rang. I have some news for you.' Smiling over at Ebony, he reached out his arm to enfold her against his side, so close that she could hear Vicki's chatter.

'Have you?' she was saying. 'Well, it'll have to wait a sec, because I've got some news of my own and I think I'd better get it over with first.'

'Don't tell me you've left Alistair again,' he sighed. 'Or has he left you this time?'

'Neither. I know this might come as a shock after all I've said about marriage and stuff, but it seems I made a big boo-boo with my pill a couple of months back and...well...the upshot is I'm going to have a baby and Alistair insists we get married straight away. I told him he didn't have to, but he's gone all strait-laced on me since going to work for you. He's threatening to get his hair cut and start listening to classical music if I don't marry him. Well, I ask you, what's a poor girl to do?'

Alan and Ebony both had to cover their mouths to smother their laughter, the result being an awkward silence.

'Alan? Are you still there? Speak to me, for heaven's sake!'

Alan gulped a couple of times before continuing with a straight face. 'That's wonderful news, Vicki. I couldn't be happier. And I'm sure Mother will be thrilled.'

'Are you sure? I thought she'd be appalled. I mean, she never liked Alistair much, but he has changed, you know.'

'I do know. I'm very pleased with his work.'

'You are? Goodness! Well, maybe he has really changed, then.'

Alan's eyes softened as they travelled over his beautiful Ebony. 'Love changes everything, Vicki, don't you know that?'

'Why, Alan, what a romantic thing for you to say!'

'Maybe I've changed too, sister, dear. Maybe I'm in love.'

'You, Alan? I don't believe it. You're not the type. Besides, who would be stupid enough to fall in love with a workaholic like you?'

Ebony took the receiver out of his hands. 'Me, Vicki.'

'Ebony? Is that you?'

'It is indeed.'

'But...but...but...'

'Perhaps you and Alistair had better come over to the house, Vicki. I'm sure your mother will want to talk to you at length.'

Ebony hung up, and, snaking her arms around Alan's waist, pulled him close. 'Your sister was speechless with delight.'

'So I heard.'

'Give her ten minutes and she'll be knocking on the front door.'

'Ten? I'll give her eight.'

'Did I hear the telephone?' Deirdre said on coming back into the room.

'It was Vicki,' Alan informed her.

'Vicki! Why didn't you call me? I wanted to speak to her.'

'Don't fret. She's coming over. She has some good news for you.'

'Vicki has some good news? Did you tell her *your* good news?'

'We did.'

'And?'

'She was...surprised.'

Deirdre grinned. 'I'll bet she was.' Her grin faded to a puzzled expression. 'I wonder what her good news is? Do you know?'

'We do.'

'Can't you tell me what it is?'

'Should we, Ebony?'

She nodded.

'You're going to be a grandmother, Mother.'

'Well, I already suspected that might be the case, but I... Oh, my God, you mean Vicki. Vicki's having a *baby*?'

'That she is,' Alan announced with a wide smile on his face. 'And Alistair is insisting she marry him. So I think, Mother, we might plan a double wedding in the near future, don't you?'

Deirdre looked as if she might pass out for a second, then rallied. She looked from Alan to Ebony to Alan again, tears glistening in her eyes. 'A double wedding,' she choked out. 'Who would have believed this a week ago? Oh, I must be the luckiest person in this whole world.'

'No, Mother,' Alan refuted, loving blue eyes gazing deeply into shining black ones. 'That honour definitely goes to me.'

HARLEQUIN PRESENTS®

Don't be late for the wedding!

Be sure to make a date in your diary for the happy event—
the latest in our tantalizing new selection of stories...

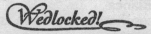

Bonded in matrimony, torn by desire...

Coming next month:

THE ULTIMATE BETRAYAL by Michelle Reid
Harlequin Presents #1799

"...an explosive magic that only (Michelle) Reid can create."
—*Affaire de Coeur*

The perfect marriage...the perfect family? That's what
Rachel Masterton had always believed she and her husband
Daniel shared. Then Rachel was told that Daniel had betrayed
her and she realized that she had to fight to save her marriage.
But she also had to fight to forgive Daniel for this...the
ultimate betrayal.

Available in March wherever Harlequin books are sold.

Yo amo novelas con corazón!

Starting this March, Harlequin opens up to a whole new world of readers with two new romance lines in SPANISH!

Harlequin Deseo
- passionate, sensual and exciting stories

Harlequin Bianca
- romances that are fun, fresh and very contemporary

With four titles a month, each line will offer the same wonderfully romantic stories that you've come to love—now available in Spanish.

Look for them at selected retail outlets.

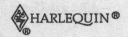

HARLEQUIN  PRESENTS®

Ever felt the excitement of a dangerous desire...?

The thrill of a feverish flirtation...?

Passion is guaranteed with the latest in our new
selection of sensual stories.

Indulge in...

Dangerous Liaisons

Falling in love is a risky affair

Coming next month:

Dark Victory by ELIZABETH OLDFIELD
Harlequin Presents #1800

Five years ago Cheska had given Lawson her heart *and* her
body *and* her soul.

So he'd loved her...and then he'd left her!

Now he was back—wanting to pick up the pieces.

Cheska might not be the same trusting and naive girl
Lawson had once known...but he seemed willing to
love the woman she'd become.

Available in March wherever Harlequin books are sold.

HARLEQUIN PRESENTS®

Harlequin brings you the best books, by the best authors!

ANNE MATHER

"...her own special brand of enchantment."
—*Affaire de Coeur*

&

LINDSAY ARMSTRONG

"...commands the reader's attention."
—*Romantic Times*

Next month:

A WOMAN OF PASSION by Anne Mather
Harlequin Presents #1797

Ice maiden...or sensuous seductress? Only Matthew Aitken guessed that Helen's cool exterior hid her passionate nature...*but* wasn't he already involved with Fleur—who just happened to be Helen's mother!

TRIAL BY MARRIAGE by Lindsay Armstrong
Harlequin Presents #1798

To outsiders Sarah seemed like a typical
spinster schoolteacher.

Cliff Wyatt was the local hunk and could have his pick from a harem of willing women. So why was he so interested in Sarah?

Harlequin Presents—the best has just gotten better!
Available in March wherever Harlequin books are sold.

BRIDE'S BAY RESORT

UNLOCK THE DOOR TO GREAT ROMANCE AT BRIDE'S BAY RESORT

Join Harlequin's new across-the-lines series, set in an exclusive hotel on an island off the coast of South Carolina.

Seven of your favorite authors will bring you exciting stories about fascinating heroes and heroines discovering love at Bride's Bay Resort.

Look for these fabulous stories coming to a store near you beginning in January 1996.

Harlequin American Romance #613 in January
Matchmaking Baby by Cathy Gillen Thacker

Harlequin Presents #1794 in February
Indiscretions by Robyn Donald

Harlequin Intrigue #362 in March
Love and Lies by Dawn Stewardson

Harlequin Romance #3404 in April
Make Believe Engagement by Day Leclaire

Harlequin Temptation #588 in May
Stranger in the Night by Roseanne Williams

Harlequin Superromance #695 in June
Married to a Stranger by Connie Bennett

Harlequin Historicals #324 in July
Dulcie's Gift by Ruth Langan

Visit Bride's Bay Resort each month wherever Harlequin books are sold.

HARLEQUIN ®

BBAYG